Slower Bear

By

Anthony Neil Smith

Fahrenheit Thirteen

By the same author.

- *Slow Bear*
- *The Butcher's Prayer*
- *Trash Pandas*

"To Brandy, love of my life, and the one who came up with Slower Bear because she's smarter than me."

CHAPTER 1

Micah "Slow Bear" Cross dug his boot heel into the man's jaw, this piece of shit named Gerardo. Slow Bear had hunted him for the last week across Nebraska. He was the whitest Gerardo Slow Bear had ever seen, his last name Prochenko. That's right. Slow Bear had spent a week in cow-country chasing a Ukrainian sex-trafficker named after a one-hit wonder.

Rico Suave.

Cold wind – March on the plains – and cold mud in the middle of this pasture, the cows around them oblivious. It had been a hell of a fight, both of them caked in dirt, each other's blood, and cow shit. But now Gerardo groaned, the boot heel grinding harder. Slow Bear caught his breath, flexed his one and only hand. He'd destroyed the fucker's nose giving him the KO, but goddamn if it didn't hurt.

Slow Bear wagged a finger at him. "I ought to… I mean, I really ought to…"

Well, Jesus, he already kicked the man's ass. What more could he do?

Gerardo writhed.

Stomp his head in? Sure, why not?

Slow Bear lifted his heel, squinted one eye to aim, and–

Hold off on that a minute.

Slow Bear had tracked Gerardo to a small Nebraskan town on a tip from another motherfucker he'd brutalized, after another tip from another motherfucker who would have trouble fucking ever again. It was a long line of tips that had led him this far, starting in Williston, North Dakota. A friend of his named Kylie – he called her "Lady" – was kidnapped by traffickers, and Slow Bear had made a mess of trying to save her. He'd even died for a few minutes before bucking up and giving it another go.

But dying once wasn't enough for Slow Bear, so he staged his own death to get away. Everyone on the rez thought he was dead. He'd faked it real good.

Being dead suited him.

In the mud, Gerardo cried ugly and angry. The wind cut through Slow Bear. Tucked in his fist was a little stun gun taken from his most recent landlady. Electro'ed the man.

How'd a one-armed man kick so many asses?

Slow Bear cheated.

Since his last trip to Williston, he'd come short of killing these punks. Murder would put him on the grid again. He didn't need that. Most of them deserved worse, though.

"You know how this works. Who do I got to deal with next?"

Gerardo huffed and puffed. Just a mess.

The smell, man. Cowshit was getting to him.

"Look, hurry this up, alright? Tell me who your boss is. I hurt you bad, but you survive. Then I'm gone."

"You… you're going to kill me." Snot and blood fucking up his face. Snorking through his broken nose. "Oh god oh god oh god oh god oh god."

Slow Bear looked away. Couldn't deal with the sight of it. Instead, he watched some cows muck around, filthy. Like swimming in a sea of fart. One big ocean of fart. All that fart gas fucking up the climate. Someone ought to fix it.

"Please, man." Gerardo wiggled under Slow Bear's heel, but his head was stuck in place. "You want money? I'll get you money. You want a girl? A young girl? An older girl? I can get you any girl you want. You want guns? I can get you guns."

"Jesus." Slow Bear sighed, pinched the bridge of his nose. "Why in the world would I chase your ass out into a field of shit and whoop up on you if all I wanted was freebies?"

"I can't tell you who—"

"Yes you can. Eventually, you all do. You can even tell him or her or whoever it is that I'm coming for them next. I don't care. Didn't help the last two guys. I *know* the last guy told you about me. That's why you slipped town so fast. And look where you are now."

He punctuated that with a grunt and more pressure.

"Name, place, twitter handle, come on."

So Gerardo told Slow Bear what he wanted to know.

Slow Bear thanked him.

Then gave him a mighty stomp that snapped his jaw like a wishbone, leaving him wailing in pain so bad even the cows were spooked.

Slow Bear started back for the highway, out of sight from where they'd ended up. A long walk. He flexed his back and shoulder and arm along the way, trying to loosen up again. Mud and shit all over him. Worst was in his hair, around his mouth. Looked at his hand. So much caked on the stun gun he wasn't sure it would work anymore. He flung it away.

All this shit was going to fuck up his car, which wasn't really his car, but Kylie's. The driver's side window had been busted out the night they took her. He couldn't afford to fix it. Then the cops had taken out the dash, the back bench and the passenger seat before he stole it back. He didn't have the chunk of change to clean the one remaining seat and the floorboards. Would probably never get rid of the odor completely, and *never* get out the mildew and mold stink from the seat getting wet in the rain because the window was busted out. Shit.

The sky looked like mean snow, the heavy wet kind. No joy to drive through. The wind nearly knocked him over as he swayed towards the road.

Gerardo still screeched way back yonder.

Fuck my life. Fuck my life.

Every day since he had 'died.' Every day.

Fuck my life.

It was a lost cause but Slow Bear didn't have any other reason to keep going.

The cars came into sight. Gerardo's sweet ride – Cadillac Escalade, black, tinted windows. Probably one of those maxed-out special editions. Leather seats, Slow Bear imagined. Gadgets up the wazoo.

Compare that to Lady's shitty little compact pulled up behind it on the shoulder, scratched and dirty, a skeleton interior. Not even sure what make and model it was. The badges had fallen off long before he came along. If he had to guess, he'd say the car was in its prime twenty-five years ago.

Slow Bear figured the Escalade would be nicer to drive than the shitty little compact, but to do that, he'd have to go back for the keys. He was already breathing rough. Took a look over his shoulder. Could still hear Gerardo, but couldn't see him.

Forget it. Too damn far to slog.

Then, from the Escalade, someone pounding on a window.

Slow Bear had missed something. Someone. Or maybe it was Gerardo's dog.

He hadn't seen Gerardo with a dog on this trip, though.

The pounding got louder. There was a rhythm to it, something a dog couldn't do. This was fist on glass.

He listened hard, heard voices shouting from inside.

Slow Bear walked to the Escalade, carefully, still not sure if this was an ambush. But if Gerardo had help, why had he run off across the field?

He reached for the back door handle. Pulled. Locked.

The pounding grew faster, louder. The voice inside finally clear: "Help us, please help us."

Whoa. That was a kid's voice.

Slow Bear grabbed the driver's door handle. Unlocked.

Two voices.

Young voices.

Girls.

He looked inside. A sheet of Plexiglas divided front and back, like in a cab, but crude. Improvised. All scratched up, dirty. Through the murk, Slow Bear saw the girls, but not clearly.

Child locks. That's why they couldn't get out.

Slow Bear pressed the unlock button. Tried the door again. Easy-peasy this time.

The girls caught their breaths at the sight of him close up. Covered in shit, one arm, some sort of Rob Zombie character. They scrambled backwards, across the bench to the opposite door.

"No, no, wait! It's fine now, it's all fine."

It didn't help much, both wide-eyed and shivering, both in barely anything – shorts and t-shirts. The older girl, must be, what, maybe a teenager? When was the last time Slow Bear had been around kids? She shielded the younger one – crap, like grade-school age – who looked over the teenager's shoulder. Both brown-skinned, but the older was Latino and the younger Sioux.

Slow Bear put his hand on his hip and shook his head. "You girls, um… you speak English?"

Winced. *Of course they do. They were yelling for help.*

The younger girl nodded, the older one still stared, burned a hole through his guts easier than orange juice did.

"This guy," Slow Bear thumbed over his shoulder, then pointed to the driver's seat. "A friend of yours?"

The younger one shook her head, but her defender hissed, "Stop it!"

Slow Bear took it in, let the girls alone a moment.

He knew Gerardo was one of the traffickers, on the road a lot, but these two were the youngest he'd seen. Just kids, for fuck's sake. Rico Suave hauling them cross country to sick fucks who'd make them do terrible things no girls that age should do, or sell them by the hour to men who should know better, but had a clump of steaming cow shit where other folks had hearts.

All this time on Gerardo's tail, the bastard had kept these two hidden well.

Slow Bear realized what he had to do, no other option in this godforsaken heartland.

Fuck.

He leaned against the doorframe, dipped his head. "That guy, I just broke his jaw. So it's up to you. Come with me, things'll be alright. Stay here and wait for him, I don't know, y'all."

To the older girl, he could tell the way she stared at him, Slow Bear didn't look like a good bet. She must've learned more about men, about lies, about staying alive, in her how-many-teen years than many women twice her age.

He added, "Promise. You'll be safe with me."

Another long moment stunk up the air between them. She finally nodded but still kept herself in front of the younger girl.

Slow Bear turned to Kylie's car. Damned thing didn't have any seats. He looked at the Caddy. Fucking sweet ride, even if he did have to muck it up.

He checked the ignition. Push-button. He got in, stepped on the brake, and pushed the button.

Nope.

Dropped his head. Climbed out.

To the girls, "Got to get the key. Stay here."

Slow Bear started back across the pasture, his legs barely there.

He wasn't ten feet from the Caddy when the older girl shouted, "I think I'm pregnant."

Slow Bear stopped, closed his eyes. Then opened them again, and kept on going.

CHAPTER 2

Being dead suited Slow Bear.

The only bad thing was his money was trapped. His settlement, his savings, all electronic: if he touched it, they'd sure enough find him, and *that* he didn't need.

He blew through his emergency stash pretty fast on food, gas, info, condoms and orange juice. Only God knew where it would all end up. Probably in a rich white man's pocket.

There was a guy Slow Bear had arrested once in Williston. Oren H was there for the oil boom, but not working in the fields. He was a computer guy, helping launder ill-gotten, filthy damp cash – whore money, meth money, even fucking heroin money – until it became clean numbers in secret accounts all over the world. Some of that cash had been trafficker money, and that led Slow Bear to slap Oren around until he promised to fuck up their accounts, steal their money, and put them on the government's radar screen.

Which meant Oren had to run for his life. But he was good at that. Dude was gay, flaming, loud, Nordic-white and bald but could still disappear in a crowd.

But Slow Bear always knew how to get in touch with him. It was easy – Oren does favors for Slow Bear, Slow Bear doesn't tell the now-less-rich trafficking bastards where Oren is.

So Oren sent him a fresh driver's license, social, and a credit card. Still Slow Bear managed to fuck up and get that card canceled at a Texas Roadhouse steak joint, getting out only minutes before the cops showed up.

Flash forward a few weeks after the fake death thing and Slow Bear was driving away from a hanger on an airfield that had doubled as a brothel and weigh station for girls being trafficked out west. In his rearview, smoke bloomed out the ceiling, leaving a lot of bad men in bad pain, a lot of ladies without a source of income or free dope, but away from a son of a bitch named Santana. Maybe they'd make it out, maybe not.

As for Santana?

Best not ask what happened to him.

The night before he found Gerardo, Slow Bear stayed the night with a new "landlady." He'd forgot how many one-night stands it added up to. She was usually the next to last in the bar at closing time, falling easily for his sad-eyed and one-armed story.

Like Jenn in Spearfish – drunk but hyper white girl, would be pretty with a different shaped head, but she made up for it with a short dress and toe rings.

Like Dawn in Granite Falls – Sioux, thirty-three, worked the cashier's window at a casino. She'd had a bad day, her boss threatening to fire her. Again. She took Slow Bear home, said she lived with her Mom, had two kids, but that they slept hard so he could really whoop it up if he wanted. Turned out they didn't sleep *that* hard.

Like Fergie in Council Bluffs – Korean (adopted by rich white people), chunky, liked fruity drinks, liked to bitch about her friends as if she wished they were dead. Nineteen. She took him back to her dorm room. She fell asleep halfway through blowing him, so he helped her into bed, climbed into her roommate's, who was gone home for the weekend anyway.

And more. Fuzzy nights. Couple fun nights. Couple of bad arguments. Lot of sad nights. As long as he got enough sleep to keep his battery charged.

The pickings were slim last night – something about a new flu going around, keeping everyone home – but this one was still a sight prettier than some he'd rode home with along his way. She thought he was an out of luck roughneck now trying to odd-job his way back home across the country. Truth was he could never go back nor wanted to nor would ever want to… until the moment he did. You never knew.

This was a white woman, sixty-years-old, but sixty now didn't look like sixty when Slow Bear was a boy. Sixty used to be old. Now, sixty was something else. Sixty could even be pretty, in the right light. Sixty wasn't front porch rocking material. That night, sixty was horny.

Smoked cigarettes at the bar, only smiled when being sarcastic. She had hair red as a bonfire, had to be dyed. Not much make-up, enough to bring out her eyes and lips. Tight jeans and strappy sandals, faded Brooks & Dunn tour t-shirt that showed her shape. She was short.

He said, "Brooks and Dunn. Haven't heard them in a long time."

"You'd better have a good story about that arm."

"It's not a good one."

She shrugged. "Any story will do."

Slow Bear felt sad for her, then for himself. He'd been trolling for easy pussy for weeks now. Or was it months? Fucking women he didn't really want to fuck for a free bed and a couple free meals. Some of those women were okay with that. Some still asleep as Slow Bear slipped out the next day. Others could get clingy real fast because, goddamn, being lonely hurt.

Slow Bear and the sixty-year-old redhead talked and drank. Slow Bear had thought he was done with drinking, but none of these ladies would've trusted him if he wasn't at least half as drunk as they were. He stuck to light beer mostly. When he needed to sink lower faster, a couple shots of Southern Comfort or some other cheap rail liquor sent him plummeting. Always been a lightweight.

Sixty said she was Abeline, a name Slow Bear had never heard before. She'd been married three times, divorced all three. Her last live-in man friend had left two years ago. His job was to travel around the country for shutdown projects.

"Then he left for something in Canada, supposed to be gone a month. After seven weeks he texted to say he wasn't coming back, and to mail him his things. I boxed them up, took them out back and set fire to them. Never heard from him again, never asked about his shit."

"That's one way to do it."

"The man claimed he made over a hundred grand a year, but he stayed at my shitty house, ate my food, and would only splurge on me at the Indian casinos. Should've known." She stabbed out her cigarette and blew smoke into the air over Slow Bear's head.

"How long ago was that?"

"Four years."

"Four years?"

"And I'll tell you the truth." She leaned closer. Vanilla vodka on her breath. "Haven't touched one cock in all that time. I swore off men."

"That right?" His hope started to dim. Might be sleeping in the car again, which was worse than sleeping on nails.

A twinkle in her eye. A hint of a grin. "Well, I tried, anyway."

Abeline slid off her stool, laid down cash for the drinks and waved good night to the bartender.

She started towards the door and Slow Bear started looking around for plan B, but he'd spent too much time on plan A. Nobody conscious left. He rubbed the spot on his back that always hurt, worse after a night sleeping in the car.

Abeline pushed the door open. Stopped, turned around. "Take a hint, boy. Are you coming with me or not?"

He slipped off the stool and rushed after her.

Slow Bear followed Abeline to her small bungalow at the edge of town, soybean fields stretching behind it. Inside, creaky, full-throated wood floors. Leather furniture. A kitchen that couldn't decide if it was 1940 or 2020. On thru to the bedroom – queen bed, unmade, Walmart comforter with a classy golden design – something Britishy.

She clicked on the bedside table – a soft light filtered through a red lightshade, turning them both to devils. Abeline took her clothes off fast, told Slow Bear to do the same. Naked and not shy, she climbed onto the bed and reached across to grab him. Her breasts swung, not large, just tired. She kept her bush tidy. She had old lady neck, but the rest of her body was in nice enough shape.

Abeline knew what she wanted, asked for it if she wasn't getting it. Slicked them both up with lube. Slow Bear asked about a condom and Abeline said, "Fuck your condom. Just fuck me."

He spent the next twenty-six minutes doing that.

Something about her got him rock hard. The cougar vibe? Her fried voice, sounded like a barfly in a Western? Whatever it was, he was glad he met her. The sheets felt nice.

Missionary was hardest for Slow Bear. He had a hard time balancing. She said, "Let's do doggy-style," like she was seventeen instead of sixty. Slow Bear got a better grip, holding tight so he wouldn't slip out of her overly-lubed pussy. She talked dirty while he pounded her. "Yeah harder, Chief, fuck me harder, fuck me harder, Chief, keep fucking me, you one-armed brave, you. Don't stop til, don't stop til, you son of a bitch. God*damn*, your cock, boy."

They ended up on the edge of the bed, Abeline straddling Slow Bear, pistoning up and down while rubbing her clit, the dirty talk now grunts and hard breaths. She kept her eyes open. He liked the way her lips looked. The lines around her mouth and eyes made the whole thing feel dirtier. It smelled worse than usual, that musky blend of man, woman, sweat, and lube topped with cigarettes and a sickly sweet Glade plug-in, fake melon maybe.

She whispered, "Come in me. Do it. Come in me."

Slow Bear did it. He let out a noise from deep inside. A moose cry.

After, they laid together on top of the golden comforter, Abeline's leg tossed over Slow Bear's junk, her rough toes rubbing his leg. She'd picked the side with no arm. He couldn't pull her in for a cuddle, but maybe she liked it that way. Spiraled her finger in his chest hair.

"Were you okay with me saying what I said?" she asked.

"Said what?"

"You know that shit about, Chief and brave? Was that too much?"

He hadn't cared. If she had been, say, a white man, and they weren't in the middle of fucking, okay. Could have got his hair raised, then. He shrugged. "No biggie. Fine."

"I'm not racist or anything."

"Didn't say you were."

"It was the heat of the moment."

Abeline laid her head on what was left of his shoulder. His phantom limb tried and failed to hug her.

"This was good," he said. "You know how to do it."

"Helps when you can keep it hard as long as you. Jesus, wore me out, son."

Don't call me 'son,' hon. "Sleepy. Fine if I stay?"

"Sure."

"I know we don't know each other so good, but, maybe a couple nights?"

She nuzzled in. "Honey, I'm up for more of this if you are. Not like anything in this house is worth stealing. So why don't you tell me the real reason you're on the road?"

"Scout's honor, I swear."

"You don't know shit about scout's honor."

He lifted a three-fingered salute to his eyebrow. "Eh?"

"Come on, tell me a story. Tell me you're not just fucking your way across the country for the hell of it. That there's a reason."

Slow Bear didn't want tell her. Felt like it would go bad. That this one was smarter than the others, had a thicker skin – literally – than the others, and probably wouldn't like the truth all that much even though she thought she would. If he refused, she might kick him out. If he told her, she might kick him out.

He turned to her, felt his cock stirring again under her thigh, and said, "I'm chasing bad guys."

Abeline raised up on her knees and scooted down the bed. She lowered her head over his crotch and said, "Tell me about it."

Not even twenty-four hours later, Slow Bear knocked on her door. She was expecting him because he told her he would be back – even though he never knew on this trip if he'd keep his promises or not. Words, only words, to get him from sundown to sunup.

She shouted, somewhere in the back of the house. Could've been *come in*, or *fuck off*, or *let me get dressed*. Didn't matter. He tried the door and it opened to Abeline coming down the hall in shorts and an oversized, stretched-out sweatshirt for Welsher Solutions – probably left over from the ex. Cigarette in two fingers, trailing smoke. She smiled when she saw Slow Bear, but then frowned when she saw the two girls standing behind him.

"Well, well, who do we have here?"

Slow Bear held his hand over each in turn, oldest first. "Pia and Melody."

Abeline leaned over, hands on her knees, closer to their faces. Her grin was back. "Yours?"

"No."

"Nieces?"

"No. Listen–"

"Can we talk a minute?" Abeline stood straight again, the worry lines on her face working overtime.

Slow Bear motioned for the girls to go in ahead of him, and Abeline didn't protest. Once they were in, Abeline shut the door leaving her and Slow Bear alone on the front steps She got a good whiff of him and wrinkled her nose. "Jesus Fuck! You been rolling in cow shit?" She shoved him in the chest. "No! No, no, no. I should've known, Jesus, too good to be true."

"Would you hear me out?"

Abeline was one tight ball of pissed-offedness. "Who are those girls? Why are they here?"

"Remember, I told you last night? Chasing bad guys?"

She rolled her eyes and flicked ash. "Bullshit."

"Well, I caught one."

"*Bull. Shit.*" A glance over his shoulder at his new ride on the curb. "And all of the sudden you've got a Cadillac, too. I don't want no part of it."

"The girls, they're in trouble. Was hoping you could help, call the police, or something. They were kidnapped. I think. Get them back home, that's all I'm asking."

"Wait. Kidnapped? You *kidnapped* them?"

"Not me. The bad guy. Can I use your shower? We'll talk after that. Look at me."

Abeline stabbed her cigarette at him. Little close to his eyes. "Like fuck. You're lucky I haven't shot you dead on my lawn already. You had your fun. Get your sorry ass on down the road or the police'll do it for you."

He grabbed her by the shoulders. Phantom limb, though. He gripped one shoulder. "I want to take a shower. I want to change my clothes. I want you to feed those girls, let them take a nap or something, and we'll talk. I told you, I chase bad guys."

She pulled away. "That make you the good guy?"

"Better than the bad ones. Give me a chance?"

Goddamn, she was mad. He liked the spark in her. Wished it wasn't directed at him. Odds are she still wouldn't buy his story, but he would like to get that shower before he had to deal with that.

Another long moment on her front steps surrounded by potted plants that had died last fall, sat through winter. He looked around. Birdfeeder, empty. Birdbath, empty. Abeline's own car in the drive. A detached garage off to the side, probably full of crap.

Abeline took a big puff and sighed out smoke. "You got clothes?"

"Yeah."

"Because I sure as hell am not washing this shit. Ruin my Whirlpool."

"You won't have to." Slow Bear wasn't sure if he had any more socks, though.

Shook her head, stepped to the door and opened it. "Alright. You know where the bathroom is."

He started down the hall without a word.

She shouted behind him, "Use the old towels!"

CHAPTER 3

It took Slow Bear a half-hour to feel even partway clean again, longer to get the stink off. He watched cow shit clump and melt on the tub floor, swirl into the drain, leaving filth trails everywhere. Hot, hot water. Stinging. He'd started with a half bar of Dove soap, but it had lathered away to nearly nothing, a dark nub in his palm. He hadn't cut his hair in months, and it was a tangled mess. Hadn't shaved since two weeks ago when he borrowed a dull razor from his one-night stand and cut himself six, seven, shit, fifteen times. Wasn't eager to do that again, so he scrubbed his beard hard, scratched off some pimples.

He climbed out feeling more human. About as human as he could feel these days. Put on his other – now only – pair of jeans. White v-neck tee and a UND sweatshirt over it. He'd never been to the University, just got a good bulk deal on UND shirts at a Goodwill before leaving the state. He would have to wear the same shitty shoes, unfortunately, but once the muck dried, he'd get most of it off. For now, they were on the front steps in the cold wind.

He wiped steam off the mirror, but it fogged right back up. He combed his hair back straight. Tossed the old bath towel on the floor.

He peeked in on the girls, eating cinammon roll Pop-Tarts at the dining-room table. They were laughing, goofing a little with each other. Chewing Pop-Tart and showing it to each other on their tongues. Crumbs everywhere. They looked up at him. Sheepish. He went on past into the kitchen, checked the fridge. Thankfully, Abeline was an orange juice drinker. He found a glass and poured some out of the carton, took a couple big gulps of it. Light on the pulp. But it was good. *Real good.* Refreshed better than almost anything, right up until it turned into molten lava in his stomach.

Slow Bear found Abeline in the living room, smoking. She flicked ash into a Dr. Pepper can on the end table. Looked like she'd missed a couple times before. Her front curtains, Kmart brash, were wide-open, gray light streaming in. She stared out as if Slow Bear wasn't in the room.

He sat in the recliner. His nose itched because of her cigarette smoke. He'd never cared much for smoking, unless it was meth but that was many months and miles ago. He'd cleaned up from heroin, the toughest one to shake. Tried to keep clean from booze too, but he had to use it like a tool sometimes. Not often, but when the alternative was waking up with a grief hangover some chemical interference was pretty damn welcome.

"Well," he said, since Abeline wasn't going first. "Thank you, first off–"

"Why are these children in my house, eating my food? Who are they? What right do you think you have…" She trailed off, another puff. Shaking her head.

"No right. None at all. Let me explain."

"Sure as shit better."

Slow Bear let out a deep breath, leaned forward in the chair. "This guy I was looking for. I found him. These girls were with him. They were on their way to something bad."

"Seriously." She didn't sound serious.

"Yes, seriously." Lowered his voice. "Those girls had been bought and sold. Either by their mommas for meth, or picked up outside of school, or slipped away from a group home. Seen it done before. Pick them up, right in front of their houses sometimes."

"Who're you, anyway? Johnny Law?"

"Not anymore."

"Not what I expected to wake up to."

Neither did Slow Bear. He never knew what to expect the next morning. "I've got to go soon. I've got to find the people these girls were sold to until I stopped it. I'd like you to do me a favor."

Another puff of the cigarette. Abeline's fingers shook. The angry lines on her face had started to soften. "Jesus Christ."

"Maybe, I don't know, get them some nice clothes, keep them safe for a bit."

"You've got to be kidding. Fucking kidding me."

"I don't know what else to do. Call the police? Me? You don't understand. That's not…" He scratched his nose. "I just can't. Trust me."

"They're after you, too? Shit, son, what have I gotten myself into?" She turned to him. Crossed her legs and propped her elbow on her high knee. Cigarette smoke like incense from an idol. "I've got two kids, all grown. Oldest is forty-one, my Sherrie. Then Gabe is thirty-nine. I've got four grandkids. Me. Can you even? Oldest one of them is a junior in college. I haven't heard from her in six months. Too old to call her own grandma, or not old enough yet. Got a sixteen-year-old grandson, used to love coming down here on weekends. Last time I called him on his birthday, every answer was, 'Alright' or 'I dunno.' I mean…" She shrugged. "Don't do this to me. I can't."

"Please, just one thing, and I'm out of your hair. Out of your life. Tell them you found the girls in the park. Get someone to send them back home."

"No!" From behind them.

They turned around. The oldest girl, Pia, stood in the doorway, with Melody behind her. Had to have heard everything.

"You alright, sweetie? You need something?" Abeline slipped right back into grandmothering.

Look at them. Pia said she was already pregnant, must've hit puberty way too early, her legs and hips beginning to take shape. Melody was sticks and twigs, flyaway hair, goosebumps. God only knew what they'd been through. Jesus, Slow Bear remembered what he'd seen back in North Dakota, back at Santana's whorehouse. Thank God, none of them had been kids. But that was only because he reserved those girls for 'special' customers. VIPs. Handle with care. Gave him a headache.

Pia balled her fists. "You can't take me home. I won't go back."

"You don't want to see your mama?"

"My mama didn't want me. Made me be with her man friend. I didn't want to. Then he took me to another man. They gave me shots. Then I was with Mr. Gerardo."

Abeline melted. "Oh, sweetie."

Slow Bear beckoned them closer. Melody stepped from around Pia, small careful steps until she was standing a few feet from Slow Bear.

"What about you? Do you want to go home?"

Melody looked at the carpet. Shrugged.

"Do you know where home is?"

Shook her head. "Mama died. I miss her."

Pia spoke up. "She was in foster care. A religious house. Something like fifteen kids, she hardly got anything to eat."

"She told you?"

Pia nodded.

"You knew her before."

"No. Met her this week, with Mr. Gerardo."

Slow Bear shifted towards Abeline. Lifted his eyebrows. Her lips were parted, not sure what to say but wanting to say something.

She finally cleared her throat. "Sweetie, what do you want to do? You want to stay here for a while?"

Melody lifted her hand, pointed at Slow Bear.

Pia stepped closer now. "We want to stay with him. Wherever he goes."

"Sorry girls, but you can't go where I'm going."

"What if they find us here? What if they try to take us back?"

He chinned towards Abeline. "She's got a gun."

"Jesus, Micah." She stubbed out the cigarette and motioned for the girls to come sit with her on the couch. Pia did. Melody eased closer to Slow Bear and rested both of her arms on his leg. She squeezed.

This wasn't going Slow Bear's way.

He brushed her out of his way and stood up. "Miss Abeline here's going to take care of you a little while. Then, we'll see. But I've got to go. People to see. Business. Grown-up business."

He turned his back on them and headed for the door. Barefoot and all. Stopped outside to slip on his shit-caked shoes, some of it hard as concrete now, going to rip his feet to shreds.

Wasn't even halfway down the drive before Abeline called out behind him, "Son of a bitch, you get your ass back in there."

"Can't. You're smart. You'll know what to do."

"Turn around. Look me in the eyes."

He kept walking, tossed his hand in the air like, *Fuck off.*

"Micah, you'd better–"

Slow Bear stopped. Abeline ran into his back. He made a slow circle, looked down at her, clutching her sweatshirt like she it was a robe.

"I done told you, boy, I can't take care of those girls."

"Just, I don't know, get them some help."

"What sort of help? A fucking rape kit? Mental help? You heard them. Good Lord, how am I supposed to help them?"

Slow Bear put his one hand on his hip, wondered what the neighbors had to be thinking. They sure as fuck were watching, he thought.

"Pia says she's pregnant."

Whatever was on the tip of Abeline's tongue died there.

"Yeah, she says she's pregnant, and how the hell am I supposed to deal with that?"

"Oh Jesus."

"Yeah."

She puffed her cheeks. "Ho boy. Poor child."

Petered out of things to say.

Which was good, because Slow Bear saw a car coming their way down the road. Out here, houses pretty far apart, it was weird to see the car prowling towards them at such a low speed, motor a low rumble. It was a Dodge Charger, red. Shiny. Closer still. North Dakota plates.

Slow Bear eased in front of Abeline, shielding her. "When I told the girls you got a gun, you do, right?"

"What?"

"If I tell you, then run. Get the gun. Shoot anyone tries to come inside."

"My God."

Closer still.

Brum-rum-rum. Brum rum-rum.

Dude in the passenger hung his arm out the window, empty-handed. He was white. Goatee. Wore a trucker-cap. Sunglasses. Glared at Slow Bear and Abeline. Hard to see the driver. Thin face, thin neck. Buzzcut. That was all.

How? How the fuck did they–

Slow Bear cut his eyes to the Escalade.

GPS.

Shit, of course.

The Charger slowed even more as it closed in on the Caddy. Drove past it, the dude in the passenger seat giving them a high chin, a two-finger wave.

Then they sped up, not by much, and were gone.

Abeline's hands gripped his shoulders. "Who were they? What was that?"

He turned to her. "You trust me?"

"Why would you ask me that?"

"Go inside, pack yourself some clothes, say, several days. I'm serious. And we've got to take your car."

Parted lips. She was already small, looked smaller. "This ain't real. This ain't happening. I never should've… I had no idea."

"We don't have time. I'm sorry, a thousand times sorry, but goddamnit, woman, we've got to go."

They hurried up the walk to the front door, opened it. The girls were right there waiting.

Slow Bear rolled his head back, looked straight up. Whispered, "Fuck."

CHAPTER 4

There they were – Slow Bear, Abeline, Pia and Melody – on the road heading west in Abeline's Saturn L-Series, a twenty-year old car that she bought eight years ago. Slow Bear did the driving because he was the only one who knew where they were going. Melody had fallen asleep and snored like a pug, while Pia stared out the window at cow field after goddamn cow field. Gray dirt, gray sky, the highway rising in front of them. In the rearview, Slow Bear saw how far they'd climbed, not realizing it. Heading into the mountains. Next stop Denver, the mile-high city.

Before that, they stopped at a big box store, good for clothes, car parts, toys and groceries, whatever you needed. Bet it had once gleamed, brand new savior – jobs and cheap shit – but now looked as filthy as everything else in this part of the world.

A mostly empty parking lot. Abeline said, "I'll be damned. That's weird."

A quick trip inside for snacks, clothes for the girls, socks and shoes for Slow Bear. Looked like a tornado had passed through. Empty shelves, usually full. Basic stuff taken for granted, like toilet paper and frozen pizzas, gone, just gone. Instead of plastic water bottles, they ended up with expensive glass bottles of French water, the only kind left.

Abeline paid for it all with her credit card, didn't raise a fuss about it with Slow Bear. Same when he stopped to fill the tank. Not a peep. Slow Bear felt shitty about it. All that settlement money he'd left behind, he could've paid for everything easily. He'd barely touched it when he had his trailer on the rez. He didn't need much. What he wouldn't give to tap into it now. He'd have to call Oren somewhere up ahead, get him to wire some cash.

They passed Kylie's abandoned piece of shit car, right where he'd left it. Think Gerardo had found his way out of the cow pasture? Or maybe he was still out there, cracked jaw and all, flopping in the mud.

Either way, fuck him.

Abeline looked over her shoulder. "You girls like music?"

Pia looked a little shocked to be spoken to at all. "Um, like, Cardi B? The Weeknd?"

"What're those?"

"Singers, like, you know?"

Abeline chuckled. "I think I stopped learning singers about nineteen ninety-nine. Do you know Garth Brooks?"

Pia shook her head.

"Shania?"

Pia shook her head. "I like rap, too."

"Well, let's see what we've got."

She turned on the stereo, currently set to a country station, some twangy guy with a smooth r&b backing track. Slick. But Abeline found a pop station, panned the speakers to the back.

An excuse for her to talk to him without the girls hearing.

"Okay, spill."

"Isn't it a little late for that?"

"This is on my dime, I ought to know the details. Like, who were those guys in the car?"

"Those guys would've come back later with more guys. Would've killed you and me and taken the girls."

"How is this real? How is this not TV?" She tossed up her hands, let them flop into her lap. "How did they even find you? They follow you?"

"The Cadillac. Bet they had a GPS on it. Only thing I can think of."

"You led them right to me."

"How the hell was I supposed to…?" *Bring it back down. She's more scared than pissed.* "I didn't know. Just wanted to get these girls some place safe. If that car hadn't showed up right then, I'd have left them with you."

"My God, and then they'd show up after you left?"

"I mean, if they were tracking the Caddy–"

"Enough, alright? Shut up." Her hands on her lap, fingers scratching fingers, the woman dying for a cigarette.

He let the tension hang a little longer. The music was awful, some sort of mumbly rap. The girls were alert, though. They knew Slow Bear and Abeline were kinda sorta fighting. Bringing more shit into their already very shitty lives.

Quietly, to Abeline, "We're going to Denver. Ever been?"

"No."

"Me neither, but I hear it's a mile high and surrounded by mountains. That's where these girls were headed when I found them. I've got to find the people who're waiting there to pick them up."

"Well, Jesus, why do you want to go and do that?"

"I'm looking for someone. Friend of mine. She doesn't deserve to be tied up in this. I owe her."

"Another young'un? Like these?"

"No, no, I mean, she's like twenty."

"How did she–"

"Wrong place, wrong time. They take who they want. Just take them. They kicked my sorry ass when I tried to stop them. Nothing I could do."

"How do you know she's… I mean, do you think she's okay?"

One shoulder shrug. "I'm dying to find out."

She switched which hand she scratched. "Can we stop soon? I've got to pee."

Maybe she really needed to. Maybe she wanted to smoke. Maybe she wanted to run like hell.

Slow Bear said, "Hope you can hold it."

They stopped at truck stops to piss or smoke or buy chicken fingers and fries. They made it to Denver late afternoon. The early Spring days were beginning to stretch longer, but the clouds covering the sun made it feel much later.

The mountains swelled into view, shadows at first, then, wow. None of them had seen mountains in real life, only on TV or in magazines. There was something unreal about them. The girls got tired of craning their necks after a while. Didn't take long for one mountain to look like the next, and that was that. They fell asleep in the backseat. Abeline dozed here and there. She'd smoked at all the stops so far, the odor of burnt tobacco on her stronger each time.

Slow Bear felt like he hadn't really slept since… since… good lord, since setting Santana's airfield on fire. Sure, he went through the motions. Laid his head down, closed his eyes, tried to calm his breathing. Maybe some nights he made it to the edge of dreaming, always jolted back by the thought of Kylie's eyes behind her glasses, or her chubby ass, or the last he saw of her, dragged away by some sick motherfuckers while their friends went to town on Slow Bear.

He shook it off, sipped lukewarm French water, and checked the address he'd gotten off Gerardo. He was looking for a Carl's Jr. Gigantic fucking burgers, Slow Bear remembered, real heart-stoppers that would make you slap your lover if she stood in your way of getting one.

Slow Bear didn't want these girls anywhere near the people here to pick them up, most likely couriers paid to hand them over to the real sickos for cash. Fuck no. They'd probably chosen this place to make it look more like a divorced dad dropping off his kids for Mom. No drama, nobody paying any mind. Most fast-food joints were in the middle of busy roads or on the edges of shopping centers, so he'd park a bit farther out and walk the rest of the way. Let them all nap while he went in and got down to business. Shouldn't take long to bust some heads and squeeze out the next name on the list.

But he was tired. The road, the fights, the fucking, they'd got to him. He didn't know how much longer he could go on without hibernating.

Abeline snorted, woke up, but pretended not to. What a luxury.

Slow Bear drove past Carl's. Hardly anyone there. A used car lot on one side – couldn't park there or the salesjerks would swarm them – and an old Radio Shack that had been turned into a pawn shop on the other. Farther along, a Mexican joint, a medical supply store, a gas station. He turned around in the parking lot of the supply store, parked. It didn't seem like the worst place to leave them. Out of sight from the windows of Carl's. He could walk behind the buildings, come in from behind.

He turned off the engine. The heater went silent, and the windows started to frost right away. He left the key in the ignition. When Abeline woke up, she could turn it on again if she wanted.

The pointless shit you worry about before heading out to face garbage people.

Slow Bear lifted Abeline's gun from her bag and tried fitting it in his jacket pocket. No go. This thing was a monster. No clue how she handled it, or if she ever really had. A .357 revolver with a six-inch barrel. Who the fuck still used these things? He'd have to ask her how she ended up with it.

He shoved it into his waistband, the cold steel of the barrel on his lower abs like an ice pick rooting around down there. Might even stick to his skin pulling it out. That would hurt.

Hoped he wouldn't need to pull it out.

Or if he did, only to slap people around with it, not shoot them.

Eased out of the car, closed the door softly. No one stirred. If Abeline was still faking it, she sure wasn't in the mood to warn him, or wish him good luck. Nope. Sitting upright, head lolled to the side. An occasional moan or grump.

Inside Carl's lobby, the world turned upside down. There was a cloudy plastic tarp separating the front area and the dining room, a large slit through the middle. The bottoms flapped around in the wind as the door closed behind him.

The teenager behind the counter looked shocked to see him. Well, as shocked as someone could look with half his face covered by a surgical mask. This was some *Walking Dead* shit.

Slow Bear stepped to the counter, which smelled like rubbing alcohol. There was a vat of hand sanitizer by the register. Make that two – one pointed towards guests, another towards the kid working there. Slow Bear looked around the room again. More hand sanitizer vats over by the self-serve drinks area.

"Help you?"

"You… you guys open?"

"Yeah."

"Remodeling?"

"No, just, you know. The virus. I hear we might close for good tomorrow, except for the drive-thru."

Virus?

"Okay."

"You want something?"

"I'm supposed to meet someone–"

"Yeah," the kid cut in. "Yeah, they're in the dining room. Over in the back. You can't miss them."

"Wait, you know about it?"

"These people, checking on me every few minutes. 'Is he here yet? Is he here yet?' I can't even get them to buy some fries. Now you're here. Finally."

The kid's voice quivered all up and down.

"You okay?"

He shook his head. "I want to go home. I might quit. Trying to pay for my car, but I don't know if it's worth it."

Slow Bear nodded, knocked the counter for luck, and started for the dining room.

"Wait, just you alone?"

"Should I have some back-up?"

"I don't mean… you don't have any children do you?"

He said "*children*" as if it was the dirtiest thing.

"I'm all by myself today."

The guy backed towards the fryers like a turtle going back into its shell.

Slow Bear turned for the tarp between the rooms a second time.

"Sir?"

Looked over his shoulder.

"Are you sure you don't want…" The guy held out a box of surgical masks.

"I'm good."

Jesus. Gave Slow Bear the creeps.

CHAPTER 5

Slow Bear pushed through the tarp into the dining room, no clue what to expect. Tired, aching, his stomach filled with caterpillars instead of butterflies. There was the good old Carl's Jr. charm – the floors slippery with grease, no idea how it got there. Cigarette burns on the tables despite the no smoking circle on the door. An old block TV high on the wall playing the Weather Channel, muted. Two paintings. The first a watercolor of a NASCAR race. The other a homeless man sleeping in a cardboard box under a big city bridge.

What?

A really old couple sat in the very front booth by the window, both with trays full of food but neither one eating. Or moving. Or blinking.

Slow Bear turned to the back, windowless, by the restroom doors. Four people. A white woman in a booth by herself, legs crossed, arms spread out on the back of the bench. Dressed for business, black slacks and high heels and a blazer over a red silk shirt.

Three others lounged around, two sitting and one standing. A thick-bodied black guy, black t-shirt, black jeans and boots, sporting a fade like he'd found his haircut in the nineties and stuck with it.

"That ain't Gerardo."

"Well, shit. I can see that."

The other woman said, "Hey, man, then who are you?" Greek accent. Thick dark eyebrows. Sleeveless tee with a tattoo of a baby's face on her arm. A crap-looking baby. The name "Stefano" scrawled shakily beneath.

The last guy looked a bit like he could be related to Gerardo. Hoodie sweatshirt, Go Golden State Warriors! Bleached blonde hair spiking out, shellacked in gel.

The Greek Babe and the Euro Trash wore surgical masks.

Euro Trash said, "She asked who you are."

Slow Bear circled his finger in front of his mouth. "What's with the… eh?"

"You don't know? Aw, man, there's some Chinese flu spreading, a real bad one." The black guy shook his head. "I'm scared for my moms. She's already got asthma."

"It's not a flu." The white woman, had to be in her hard forties, with gray streaks in her brown hair, long but pinned up that day. "It's a Coronavirus. Where's Gerardo?"

Slow Bear walked across the dining room, wanting to keep the workers and the comatose old people out of the way if it went bad. "He's not feeling up to this. Maybe he's got this flu."

"I doubt it."

"Hey, man, where'd you lose your arm? Iraq?" The black guy asked.

Slow Bear shook his head. "Hunting accident."

He'd been hunting some asshole war criminal posing as an oil worker up on the Bakken, but the dude surprised him with a shotgun blast to the shoulder. They didn't need to know that.

The Greek stood, crossed her arms. Euro Trash stayed seated across from her. Those masks, man. All they needed were white coats and a hypodermic needle.

"Can I call him? Something to confirm your story?"

"I haven't told you a story yet. And no, you can't call him. He lost his phone."

"There are other phones."

"And his jaw. Well, he didn't lose it so much as I broke it."

He didn't mean to say it. The mask thing threw him off. The black guy marched over and clamped his massive hand on the back of Slow Bear's neck. *Squeeze.* No way to look dignified when that happened. Slow Bear's shoulders shrugged and went tight. Teeth gritted.

Euro Trash pulled out a gun. Looked like a run-of-the-mill nine. The Greek was no slouch, either, reaching behind her back and coming out with a black block of death – oh, those Glocks – a big bang in a compact frame, this one with a rail light and laser sight.

Nifty.

If the old people had noticed, they sure were quiet about it.

Slow Bear held up his hand. "I give."

The black guy reached under Slow Bear's shirt and ripped Abeline's monster gun straight out – yes, it *did* take skin with it – hefted it, then set it on the table in front of the white woman.

"Fuck's sake, man, who *are* you?"

"My name is Micah."

"Micah who?"

"No, say, 'Micah what?'"

Sigh. "Alright. Micah what?"

"Micah wants to know where you plan on sending those girls next."

The white woman and the Greek turned to each other. Clearly they were the ones in charge here, even if the Euro Trash guy thought it was him.

"You know where the girls are?"

"I might."

Euro Trash moseyed over and twisted the barrel of his pistol against Slow Bear's brow. "Listen, asshole. You're going to tell me where my brother is, and then you're going to tell me where the girls are. If you do that right now, maybe the things I do to you won't hurt so bad, you feel me?"

"I don't know your brother."

"Gerardo, idiot! Gerardo!"

"He's your brother?"

"What did I just say?"

"Older? Younger?"

"Younger. I'm telling you, if he's been hurt–"

"Okay, I can see it. How about you put the gun down first? And hey, buddy, on my neck? Can you chill? That shit hurts, man."

The dude eased off, giving Slow Bear's nerve a break.

The white lady gave him a *Well? We're waiting* look. "Where are the girls?"

"I'll tell you if you tell me where they're going from here."

"Why do you care?" Smug. Dark lipstick, heavily applied. "Are you and Gerardo trying to pull one over on us?"

"I knew I couldn't trust him." Euro Trash acted like he wanted to slam his fist into the wall, or into Slow Bear, or into *something*. "Goddamn it! He always cheated, ever since we were kids."

"Fuck no, I'm not working with your brother. I just want to know where they're going next. Name and an address. Or a number. Or a meeting place. I don't want your money."

"But you're trying to do an end-run around us? Cut out the middlewoman?"

White bitch was determined to smooth her way out of this. Everything about her showed that she was too good for this group – clothes and shoes, make-up, and the faux English-accent she was working *really hard* on.

"The truth?"

She nodded.

"Okay. I kicked Gerardo's ass and took the girls. I want to make sure none of you ever see them. Ever. And I'm going to climb the ladder to the guy who thought he could sell them in the first place, and then the guy who's paying him for them."

The haughty bitch smiled. "You so sure it's a guy? Not a woman?"

He shrugged. "Everyone's a guy to me. A guy is a guy. Right, guys?"

The Greek: "Bullshit."

"Nope. I'm a shit liar. That's the truth."

Euro Trash lifted his gun to Slow Bear's temple and–

Slow Bear slapped Euro Trash's arm out of the way and dropped to the floor like a bag of potatoes. The shot singed his hair, but it *destroyed* the black guy's nose.

The sound got sucked out of Slow Bear's ears.

He looked up. The black guy's nose was gone, gushing blood. His mouth was Jaws-wide-open. Blood and bits of nose on the table behind him. The Greek fumbled with her Glock, trying to get a bead on Slow Bear. Euro Trash freaked the fuck out, trying to get his wits back while the white bitch, standing now, shook her head at Euro Trash and waved her hands in front of her. *Noooo! Noooo!*

What a mess.

Good.

CHAPTER 6

He heard the old people shouting "My God!" and "Oh my God!" once the ringing went away. Then more shouting from the back kitchen.

The hole where the black guy's nose used to be was a geyser. Euro Trash watched, stunned.

Just enough time for Slow Bear to lunge for The Greek and pin her gun arm to her side. She fired into the floor. Slow Bear felt the heat of it on his thigh, but it missed. Once he had The Greek wrapped up, hard to do with one hand, he slipped on the greasy floor, landed on his back with the Greek on top of him.

Right on time for Euro Trash to swing his barrel towards Slow Bear, but, oops.

A bullet exploded into The Greek's hips.

Euro Trash had the Big Mo now, though, and let off three more shots *pop pop pop*.

Slow Bear went underwater again.

Bullets hit the Greek's stomach and breast, and the floor above Slow Bear's head.

The white bitch looked like she was screaming at Euro Trash, but the Big Mo continued – bastard's face screwed up and red – as he shot her in her wide-open mouth. Down she went, falling on top of Abeline's gun.

Behind Euro Trash, hard to see through the dead Greek's hair fanned over Slow Bear's face, the black guy had gushed blood all over the walls and was bouncing back and forth between the two bathroom doors like a pinball.

Slow Bear reached for the Greek's pistol. She'd lost her grip. Spidered his hand all over the floor, keeping the Greek on top of him in case Euro Trash wanted to keep plugging away. Spider to the left, spider to the right. Frantic.

Didn't see it, didn't feel it.

"Hold up, now, whoa whoa whoa. Dude?"

He still couldn't hear too well. Meaning Euro Trash probably couldn't either.

How long before cops showed up? If that happened, how long before Abeline realized he wasn't coming back? Would she go home? Would she turn the girls over to social services?

"Dude!" Slow Bear tried flagging down Euro Trash, hoping he wouldn't shoot his hand off. "Dude!"

"The fuck do you want?" Shouting at each other to be heard at all.

"Listen, I told you I have the girls, right? I do, I have them. They're close."

"Yeah?"

"So if you know the next destination, you and me, we can deliver. We can split the money."

Terrible fakeout. He didn't know how the money worked. Maybe they'd all already been paid. Or maybe it was all wire transfers. Fucking PayPal, Venmo, Apple, whatever.

Euro Trash stood over the Greek and Slow Bear. "You said you broke my brother's jaw."

"I did. He deserved it."

"I could kill you now, call it a loss and move on."

"Or you could wait until I give you the girls, then kill me. This is all a crapshoot."

He nodded. "Yeah."

The stuffiness was fading. Slow Bear worked his jaw, popped his ears. He didn't hear the black guy at first, then picked up the moaning, *motherfuckers*, and sucking air through teeth. A streak of blood where he'd slid from the wall to the floor.

Still spidering, just slower, less obvious. "Get rid of your other partner over there, and we're in the clear. Got to hurry. All the noise you made shooting up the place."

"Right, right." Thinking it over. "But my brother. You didn't kill him?"

"He's fine. He'll need his jaw wired."

Spider. His finger brushed the bottom of the grip. He tried to claw it toward him with his middle finger. Broke his fingernail. Reached more. Got two more fingernails on it.

Euro Trash paced back and forth between Slow Bear and the black guy. Every time he got near his friend, if that's what they were, the black guy would say, "Man, help me, man. Don't kill me man. Motherfucker, this hurts! Goddamn!"

Dude was leaking a lot of blood, hands covering his face, what was left of his nose clogging and spurting and choking.

Gave Slow Bear even more reason to nearly sprain all the muscles in his arm trying to grab this Glock from the floor just out of reach.

"Big money, and you'll be the only one who survived this thing. Maybe they'll give you some battle pay."

"Don't work that way."

"What's going to happen next? Going to take him to the hospital? Or call 911 and take off? Trust that he'll keep his mouth shut about you? About the girls?"

"Aw man, Petey, come on, now. Don't listen to him."

Gerardo and Petey? Guy's name was Petey? "Yeah, Petey. Don't listen to me. I'm the only person who can get you those girls.

More pacing. More headshaking. More labored breathing. "Fuck!"

Drawing a crowd. Kitchen workers with cellphones recorded through a crack in the back door. The counter kid peeked through the tarp. Shit.

The Glock. Almost in his grasp.

"Aw, Petey, I'm I'm I'm bleeding out here. I'm scared. Got to get me some help."

"Fuck, Hampton, just…" Petey detoured into the men's bathroom, came out with a wad of brown paper towels and tossed it to the black guy. "Hold this over it. We've still got business to do."

"He's going to slow you down." Slow Bear almost got a finger slipped into the Glock's trigger guard. "Business first, right? Or is this guy your best friend?"

Petey looked down at Hampton. "Got to leave with the one that brought you. Loyalty means something."

"Means you'll both rot in jail together."

Petey shook his head, set his lips hard. "You? I don't know you. I can count on Hampton."

Euro Trash Petey stepped back over, straddled the Greek and Slow Bear. "Sorry, cool guy. But I'm going to start shooting off body parts until you tell me where the girls are. The quicker you tell me, the more merciful I'll be."

"For fuck's sake, man."

"So." Petey kicked the Greek's body to the side. Aimed his pistol at Slow Bear's crotch. "Let's start with your jewels. Tell me–"

Slow Bear lifted the Glock and shot Petey until the clip emptied.

Petey was done.

Dead weight.

Slow Bear pulled his legs back before Petey crumpled across the Greek's body like some blood-soaked Kama Sutra.

A quick check to make sure he was okay. The Greek had leaked all over him, but that was fine for now. Thinking about the clock, *tick tick tick*.

He checked the three dead ones for ID. The women hardly had pockets enough to keep anything in. No purses laying around. Petey had a wad of cash in his pocket. That was fine. But nothing else. He wiped the Glock with fast food napkins that tore like crazy, tossed it near the Greek's body. No need to even bother with Petey's gun. But he needed Abeline's. He rolled the white bitch's body off the table. Bit of a shock to see how little was left of her face from the eyes down.

The eyes. They were still moving. Blinking.

Jesus fuck!

Then there was gurgling. Air bubbles in the pool of blood where her lips used to be. Slow Bear couldn't believe this shit. He leaned his ear to her chest.

Still breathing.

He recoiled, fell onto the bench across from her. Was this some sort of zombie shit?

Then her body start to seize, like she was choking. Exactly. Even if she lived through the gunshot, her lungs were filling with blood. Her body was convulsing, drowning. The creepiest goddamned thing Slow Bear had ever seen.

"Fuck."

She finally stopped flopping. Her hands stretched wide, then fell into her lap.

Slow Bear wondered if she might have survived if he hadn't turned her over. She had a clear airway until he did. Her blood coated the table, ran off the edges. All over Abeline's gun. He picked it up, took it into the men's room. He set it in the sink, turned on the tap, then tried to wash away as much blood and snot as possible.

"Aw man, you got to help me, please."

Startled Slow Bear. He'd forgotten about poor Hampton, noseless, sprawled across the entry to the bathroom, keeping the door propped open. "Man, I ain't done nothing to you except a little pinch on the neck. Look at me, I'm dying over here."

Slow Bear turned the tap off, shook the gun off. Still wet, but he wanted out of there much faster than it would take to dry.

He looked down at Hampton. "I bet you'll be okay. They can make you a new nose."

"Motherfucker, I'm bleeding out here!"

"Keep the pressure on with those towels. It's going to be okay. Now scoot out of the way so I can get out the door."

"You can't leave me here." He lifted his free hand. Shaky. "Call me an ambulance or something."

Slow Bear sighed. Shoved the wet gun back into his jeans. He hoped the water wouldn't drip and – too late. He saw the dampness spread, looked like he pissed himself.

"Tell me, Hampton. Do you know where the girls are supposed to go next?"

"Man, I only do what they tell me. Step by step, man. You hear what I'm saying?"

Slow Beer knelt in front of Hampton. "I don't know, man. I think you're still trying to hold onto some dignity, show you're a team player. Wait a sec."

He bounced up, looked around the room. He checked the white bitch's blazer pockets. Pulled out a cell phone. He knelt in front of Hampton again, held up the phone. "If you tell me where they were going next, and who they were going to, I'll leave this phone with you. If not, I'll take it with me and leave you to figure out your own salvation, buddy."

"Come on, man, I told you–"

"You told me bullshit. Give me something. Quick, now."

Hampton squinted. Weighed betraying the bosses versus saving his ass. Even then, how was he going to explain what had happened? He was going to end up a noseless snitching freak with a child trafficking charge in a shitty max security prison.

"If I were you," Slow Bear whispered, leaning in. "I'd take the easy out, get the ambulance here, and figure out the rest later."

The wad of paper towels was nearly completely soaked through. Starting to drip blood into Hampton's lap.

"Aw, man, fuck you. We're supposed to take the girls over to Salt Lake City, then someone else is taking them out to San Bernardino."

"California?"

"Yeah, man."

"Why can't one person take them the whole way? Why not just you? Or Gerardo?"

A shrug. "Aw man, it's, you know, it's about mixing things up.

Same guy with two girls across the country, on security cameras? Easier to find. If you keep switching up – new drivers, some wigs for the girls, new clothes. Sneaky shit."

"But the next stop is the next to last?"

"Yeah, man. I guess. They don't tell us much. Salt Lake City's where my boss lives." Hampton told Slow Bear where to go in Utah, who to see. He didn't know the buyer in San Bernardino. "Special order. Virgins, man. More money than I've ever made in my whole life."

Slow Bear couldn't help but laugh, even though it wasn't funny.

"What? What was that?"

Slow Bear set the phone into Hampton's bloody palm. "One of those girls? Is pregnant."

"You fucking with me?"

"Nope. Now move away from the door or I'll finish you off."

Hampton scooted out into the dining room. Slow Bear edged past him, started for the tarp. Everyone who worked there had to have been watching, only a couple with real surgical masks. One pimply kid looked like an assistant manager, had the vest and everything.

Hampton shouted, "Motherfucker! This phone's dead, motherfucker!"

The people in the lobby stepped back, taking in all of Slow Bear – the blood coating his jacket, arm, and face. Their eyes naturally sank to the gun in Slow Bear's waistband. The wet spot on his jeans.

"Better be careful. They've all got this virus. Wait for the ambulances."

He parted the crowd like a hot knife through catshit, if that was even a thing, and headed for the exit. The assistant manager trailed behind. "Sir? Hold on a sec, sir. I need to talk to you. Can you stand still, please? Sir?"

Slow Bear turned, stopped. The kid ran into his chest, bounced back. "What?"

"Sir? I'm going to get fired, sir. What do I do?"

"Wait for the ambulances, okay? I swear they're on their way."

Slow Bear left the kid standing, mouth breathing, the air sucking his mask in and out, while he pushed through the door and back out into the chilly air. No cops speeding into the parking lot. Nobody trying to make him carry the weight on this. But goddamn, all those kids had film of him now. It wouldn't take too long for the wrong eyes to see the footage and connect the dots – Slow Bear was still alive and kicking.

He turned and went back in, called out to the kid who worked the counter, "I've changed my mind. Could you spare a handful of those masks?"

Out in the parking lot, things were quieter, but for how long he had no idea. There would be cops and EMTs arriving, so he had to hurry. Bright sun and biting wind, leftover snow in the shade making its last stand. Slow Bear walked back to the car.

Which wasn't there.

Not a trace.

"That cunt."

CHAPTER 7

Maybe "cunt" was a little harsh.

Like, Abeline had agreed to drive across country with him without a lot to go on, after a one-night stand that had promised nothing more than satisfying an itch and giving them a warm body to cling to for the night. Add two girls who were in mortal danger, and that was a lot to digest.

She came anyway, in her own car, spending her own money.

If she took off while he was in a fast food joint surviving a bloodbath, killing someone he'd very much wanted not to. And *fuck fuck fuck* security cameras and cellphones. Or someone noticed the car parked there by itself, knocked on Abeline's window, scared her. Or she was overwhelmed and took the girls with her to find a way out of this shit, okay, he could understand that.

Still, that meant she'd abandoned Slow Bear to the fates. So, yeah, maybe cunt was about right.

He was about to say it again –

– when a horn honked, a couple of short stiff bursts. He looked up at the Saturn coming around the corner of the building, Abeline at the wheel, both girls looking at him, freaked out. Abeline stopped, rolled down the window. "Get in. Let's go!"

He did not need to be told twice. Got in and away they went.

The girls poked their heads over both sides of his headrest. "Are you okay? Are you bleeding? Why are you so bloody? Does it hurt? What happened? Where did you go? We woke up and you weren't here! It was scary! Where are we?"

And so on.

Slow Bear closed his eyes. "Buckle up, girls. We've still got a long drive ahead of us."

"But Miss Abeline said we could get something to eat? Like tacos. You smell bad. Like, gross. *Ewwwww!*"

"I said *sit* and *buckle up*!"

They hopped to action, got in their seats and buckled up. Slow Bear peeked over his shoulder. Both of them washed up in clean clothes, looking much too young for one of them to be pregnant. Some piece of shit *bought* them. Like they were in a catalogue. Paid extra for virgins, and probably even a little more for delivery insurance. Goddamned perv postal service.

"Where to?" Abeline gripped the wheel, eleven and one. Hunched forward.

"Just… drive for now. Let me think." Felt like he might have blood on his face. He wiped it off, looked in his hand. Clear. Probably the Greek's drool.

Abeline asked the girls, "Radio?" And all three argued Miley or Megan Thee Stallion or Shania Twain until she tuned into a hip-hop station, speakers to the back again so the adults could talk.

"We had to move. We were getting bad looks from a guy at the car lot next door. He would disappear inside for a while, then wander out again, getting closer to the car every time. And then the sirens, I thought maybe police–"

"It's okay. It's fine."

"All that blood. What happened?"

She turned out of the parking lot into the side streets around the business complex, bland brick buildings, all with the same embossed signs, none of the names a clue to what sort of business it was.

Klondike Ltd.

Strauss & Martin

Three Cats Organic

LMQI Inc.

Slow Bear imagined nearly bare offices, empty desks, one guy spinning himself in an office chair, bored out of his mind. A front for someone doing something really bad. Waiting for a call every now and then telling him to wire money to this account or that, like, payments for young girls, potent heroin, meth, maybe even snuff films.

"Did you hear me? What happened back there?"

"I had a meeting."

"A meeting?"

"I told them what I wanted. They told me they wanted the girls. I lied to them about getting the girls, trying to figure out who was next on the chain. They didn't want to tell me."

"They wanted the girls?"

"Didn't I tell you that? Listen, I got what I wanted. It took a bad turn."

"Did you… kill someone?"

He rolled his head to the side, quick peek in the back. The girls were either not listening to them talking, or they were listening *really hard*, pretending not to.

"I didn't want to. He was trying to kill me first."

Abeline's face went pale. Slow Bear thought she was going to snap the wheel in two. "This can't be real."

"There were four people, shipping little girls all over the country. That's their job. There are hundreds more like them. Thousands. I don't even know. Guy in California *bought* the girls. He's expecting them. Paid extra for virgins."

"Stop. Please, stop. This is ridiculous."

"What?"

"Jesus, are you kidding me?"

"Did you think I was kidding when I showed up at your house with them? All in good fun?"

"Well, I'm sorry if this is normal for you, not for me! I have no idea what I'm doing here. I'm scared, and you're not really helping."

Slow Bear felt a headache pounding deep in his head, someone turning up its volume with every word. "Don't freak out when I tell you this, okay?"

"I can't promise–"

"You have to. There's no two ways–"

"Fine, sure, okay, I promise not to freak out when you tell me about murdering people."

"I killed *one guy*. In self-defense. I try my goddamnedest–"

"Language!" She looked over her shoulder at the girls. Pia, smiled at her, then went back to bopping her head to rhymes dirtier than "goddamnedest" for fuck's sure.

"I try, you hear me? I used to be a cop. I've had to kill before, and I hate it. I hate hate hate it, okay? Even the absolute worst piece of shit I ever had to snuff out, as angry as I was, I still hated it. So back there, I was trying to talk my way out, but the bastard pulled his gun and wanted to shoot me in the head. I wasn't going to let him. He ended up shooting another guy's nose off."

"Oh my God!"

"Then this other one, this woman, she had a gun, so I tackled her. The dude shot her, too, thinking he was going to hit me, but he didn't. Shot her a lot."

"I need a cigarette."

"She was right on top of me. And then he shot that other bitch–"

"*Language!*"

"Let me tell it. He shot a white woman who seemed to be in charge of them all. Shot her in the face. Half her face, gone."

"Shh!"

"Then what happened?" Pia piped up behind them, scooting forward as far as she could with the seat belt on. "Is she okay, the bitch who got shot?"

"No, don't... I didn't mean to call her that. She was a nice woman." Felt sick saying it. Like swallowing someone else's spit, not in a French kiss sort of way. God knows what the highest bidder would do to them, but the white bitch would've smiled, taken the payment, and shooed the girls into his grubby hands.

"Is she okay?"

"Maybe she'll be okay. Maybe. There's always hope."

"Okay. I hope so, too."

Melody said, "Me too!" the way little sisters do, but had no clue what was going on. "Can we have tacos now?"

Abeline turned to Slow Bear. "Your call."

The gas gauge was under half a tank. They would need to stop soon enough anyway, and he was in the mood for some seven-layer Combos and a Sunkist.

"West. We're going to Utah."

CHAPTER 8

The gas station didn't have tacos, so they went a little nuts on candy instead. He told Pia and Melody to pick out three things each. He grabbed pizza-flavored Combos (no seven-layer, damn it) and Rolos and a beef stick. Sunkist in a bottle. All on Abeline's card while she pumped the gas outside, told him to get her a can of iced tea and pork rinds. He'd keep the cash from the dead traffickers a secret for now. He felt like a fucking stooge for it.

It was a bit of a ghost town. He had forgotten the masks until he piled the crappy food haul on the counter and looked up to see a thick white clerk in NASA-scientist glasses whose woolly beard was covered by a surgical mask, trying to keep far back from the till while he rang them up. Awkward as hell. A TV in the corner behind the counter played Fox News and a big graphic *Chinese Plague* on the screen besides a talking head whose voice didn't sync up with her mouth.

"*But is it like a new strain of flu, or something more sinister?*"

He told the clerk "Thanks," but the guy didn't say a word. Instantly stepped over to his vat of hand sanitizer and squirted way too much. He began rubbing his hands, eyes on Slow Bear the whole time. Gel dripping to the floor.

Pia and Melody ran outside to the car, shouting and laughing. Slow Bear took backward steps, glass doors sliding for him at the last second. Thinking this clerk might try the shotgun under the counter if they broke eye contact.

It didn't happen like that. Slow Bear stopped by Abeline's car and looked around the lot, everyone else already inside. The only other vehicle was the clerk's ancient Pontiac Sunfire that used to be blue. The interstate was eerily quiet. The cold caught up to Slow Bear now that he had a moment to stand still, inhale some icy air, and feel something like brainfreeze. He closed his eyes.

He tried to remember what Kylie had looked like that morning in the diner before she was taken. Laughing, sarcastic, lop-sided grin. Big breasts pushed up by the table edge. Enjoying a big breakfast.

Before they drugged her and enslaved her, sent her God knows where.

The only image he conjured was her terror as the motherfuckers dragged her from the car.

Their pals kicked the shit out of him, which wasn't long after he'd gotten his shit kicked out of him on the rez by an old friend.

He felt every kick. Still.

Grabbed his side.

Remembered where he was.

Not in the past. The present. Aches and pains as always, but not from steel-toed work boots this time.

"You alright, Micah?"

Sweet honey voice of Abeline, like a balm running down his head to his shoulders, arms to waist, legs to toes.

Well, not sweet honey. More like burnt sugar. Still liked it fine.

"I'm really tired."

Slow Bear stood in front of the bathroom mirror at the hotel, leaning in, face almost touching the glass. He'd taken off his clothes – ruined with blood now – and started the shower. Typical cheap hotel tub, cracked and stained by rust and minerals. He had hoped for better quality, but Slow Bear and Abeline had agreed to take the very first exit they came to with a hotel. This was that. Once a chain, you could tell, the sign long gone while a plastic banner hung across the front: *Restful Nights Hotel & Café.*

Slow Bear misread it as "Restless" at first, almost decided not to risk it. But the girls were exhausted, Melody especially. So young, no mom at home, no life to go back to. Slow Bear didn't even know her last name. Neither did Pia.

Okay, they chanced it. Half a mile from the interstate, another quarter mile to town, surrounded by remnants of a forest.

The mirror steamed up. Slow Bear wiped it clear.

He really wanted to shave. The beard was itching like ants marching over his face. He'd been shocked to see what he looked like – dead eyes after having watched two more murders and committing one himself. The images kept fucking with him: one second her face was there, the next it wasn't. Too fast. Those air bubbles when he turned her over, essentially killing her.

Dead eyes. He shouldn't have dead eyes. The traffickers in Carl's, they're the ones who should have–

His hand shook.

The mirror steamed up again. Time for the shower.

The water was too hot at first, but he gritted his teeth and let his skin get used to it pounding on his back. Stepped further into it, soaked his hair. He watched dirt and blood run down his body and splat against the porcelain. It didn't matter how clean he scrubbed himself, there was always someone standing by to cover him in filth again.

He didn't hear the bathroom door open, too busy lathering up, but soon Abeline's voice, small, sounded, "Micah?"

"Yeah?"

"You okay?"

"Starting to feel better already."

He heard some rustling, guessed she might need to pee real bad, couldn't hold it anymore. Didn't bother him. He dunked his head under the stream to drown out the noise. Being a gentleman, so he thought.

Then he felt a chill, turned around, and saw that Abeline had stripped down, pulled the shower curtain back, and was climbing in with him.

She closed the curtain again, stood huddled, arms crossed, feet tight together. "Can you move? I'm freezing."

They scooted around each other, a lot of skin on skin. Hers was tight, goose pimpled. Any question about her wanting to fuck him again, he had his answer.

Look at her, the water cascading down, her red hair shining. Some moles scattered around her back, one right in the middle of her right ass cheek. Legs, skinny. Tiny feet. The harsh fluorescent light let Slow Bear see more of her than the night before, her fuzzy red-hued lamp casting shadows. This was the body of woman who'd worked long hours at shit jobs, on her feet most of them. This was a cigarette smoker. This was rough skin, cellulite, stubble under her armpits.

She spun slowly in the stream, her head back and eyes closed, hands squeegeeing her hair. Blue veins on her chest and breasts. Barest bit of a belly.

Slow Bear felt his cock growing hard and grabbed it. He tried to tamp down what he was thinking because he was exhausted, didn't want to disappoint or turn her down. His body was automatic, though. *Pussy, man. Pussy.* Force-feeding him adrenaline.

Abeline eased against him, her head not reaching his shoulder, her back sticking to his torso. Her heels on his toes. "You don't have to hide it, big boy."

He took his hand away. Fully stiff and ready to go. She pressed her ass against him, pushed his cock up.

"Just tired is all."

"Well, one part of you doesn't feel tired." Lifted her eyes. "It doesn't have to be a marathon. It doesn't even have to be that great. But I do like the way you feel, you know."

"Mm hm."

"We can be quiet. The girls won't hear."

"You don't know that."

"You really don't want me?"

She'd hardly finished saying it when Slow Bear kissed and bit her neck. She took in a sudden breath, rubbed her ass back and forth across him.

She bent over, reached behind her, and guided him in with her fingers.

"Wait, don't we need–"

"No lube this time. I've been thinking about this for hours."

Somehow, they kept the noise down. Nice and slow until she came first, every muscle in her body tightening. She lifted her right foot and wrapped her leg around his, squeezing hard while he started to pump harder, enjoying the shape and feel and smell of her. Until…

After, they lathered each other. Slow Bear wrapped Abeline in his arm from behind.

"Jesus, boy, you know how to make that thing work."

"Thanks?"

"Shit yeah, you'd better thank me." A chuckle. "I have no idea what I'm doing. It's crazy, running away with some guy I barely know."

"Special circumstances."

"You're right. Maybe if you hadn't brought the girls… You know what? Maybe not. If you'd asked me to go with you even without them, I might've done it. There's something about you. Something worth getting into trouble for. I always do this, though, fall in with the bad men."

"There's plenty worse."

"Why am I so stupid?"

"I don't think I could've done this without you."

"Are you sure you're not a cop? Not some sort of federal agent undercover?"

"I'm just a guy. I was a cop a long time ago, but not a very good one. I'm looking for my friend who got taken by these motherfuckers. I've seen some dark shit. I want to do something about it. Probably won't make a dent, but that's all I've got left."

"How about others, like the girls? Have you, like, *saved* anyone else?"

"Hard to say. Some of the women do it because they want to. Some of them like the free drugs."

"You mean *kids*?"

"These are the youngest I've seen, but there are more out there. The rest are like my friend, even older. Most times, it's a lot easier to buy wholesale from overseas and ship the girls here than it is to find them on American streets."

"So how do they get wrapped up in it?"

"If you take a girl off the streets, by kidnapping her or promising her the world, or promising her money, free dope, there's less overhead than if you buy lump sums. Pure profit."

Abeline shivered. "Oh God. Poor things."

"It's hard for one man to compete with heroin. Maybe a whole SWAT squad can take the girls home, but some will run right back to it. Wish I knew how to put a stop to that."

"You're doing more than most."

He grinned. "You believe me? You don't think I'm bullshitting you?"

"Are you?"

"But do you believe me?"

"I don't *want* to, but I do, you know? I don't know yet."

"Trust me."

She turned in his arms, ran her fingers over the rough moonscape of skin that had once been Slow Bear's shoulder, to the smooth patch where the rest of the arm had come off cleanly. "What really happened back in Denver? How can you do everything you said you did with just one arm?"

"Practice. And luck."

"Please."

He sighed. The water was going cold, they'd been in here so long. "This guy tried to kill me. I tried to talk him out of it. He kept trying. So I killed him instead. They were wanting to make money off selling those girls to a goddamn monster in California, so now I want to take him out of this world, too. And if someone along the way can tell me what happened to my friend, well… I owe it to her. It's my fault she's gone."

"I'm sure it's not."

He didn't have an answer to that. Of course it was his fault, but he wasn't going to try to change Abeline's mind. It was nice to have a woman *like* him for the first time in a long while. Kylie had liked him plenty, sure, and definitely wanted to fuck him, but he'd said no. Something hadn't felt right about it. He hadn't expected this thing with Abeline to last longer than one night, but here they were again, and it felt really good.

"Jesus, my nipples. Ouch." She rubbed her fingers over one, sucked in air through her teeth. "Let's get out of this ice water and into bed."

She squatted to turn off the shower. Got him tingling down there again. But this time, no. He let it go, looked away. They climbed out, wrapped around some towels, and snuck out into the darkened room, except for the blasting and flashing TV, where the girls had already fallen asleep, not even under the covers of their queen bed, sprawled across each other.

Abeline said, "Let them be." She turned off the TV, and they climbed into the other bed.

He clung to her tightly, and she didn't seem to mind.

Quick glance across at the girls' bed. Pia snored.

Slow Bear hoped they had good dreams. *The devils can't get you here.*

CHAPTER 9

Slow Bear slept from eleven fifty-six until two fourteen in the morning. The glowing red numbers of the hotel clock-radio did not lie. He'd been dreaming, it evaporated when his eyes blinked open. Was he swimming? Struggling to stay above waves? In an ocean? A lake? A pool? He couldn't remember, but felt the need to take in a huge breath. So he did.

Lucky he didn't wake Abeline or the girls. First thing he heard was Pia still snoring. A glance over, the pitch black softening to shadows and shapes – a red blip from the fire alarm flashing every handful of seconds – showed that she and Melody had found their way beneath the sheets and comforter at some point while he'd been out. Still sleeping tightly against each other.

Almost as tightly as Abeline clung to Slow Bear's chest. She had worn a t-shirt to bed, an old pair of boxers. At her house, bare-assed naked, the both of them. Instant modesty around kids. The way it should be.

He tried to swallow the rock that had lodged in his throat. It wouldn't go away.

Swung his legs from under the sheets, slipped from beneath Abeline's arm. He got up, found one of the new t-shirts from Target, draped it on. Athletic shorts. Fell over trying to put those on.

Quick piss in the dark. Another check on the others to make sure they were still asleep, and then Slow Bear slipped out the door into the hallway.

Forgot his shoes. Fuck.

But he didn't mind his bare feet on the hotel carpet. Okay.

He made for the elevator. He thought about the hallways in the empty Overlook Hotel from *The Shining*. Eerie. How many of these rooms were empty? How many were haunted?

When they'd checked in, all masked up this time, the parking lot was, like every other place of business they'd passed along the way, nearly empty. Slow Bear thought in a real apocalypse, there'd be more cars left behind than this. Abandoned, or full of dead passengers, or out of gas and too far from a pump. No, this was a different End of Days. Cars parked in garages, no one trying to flee, everyone staying home.

The maskless, badly-shaven night manager had been watching a rerun of an old Final Four game because there were no fresh ones. Fuming about it to Slow Bear and Abeline. "Unpatriotic, canceling March Madness. Especially in this real madness, people need a break right?"

"Aren't you worried about getting sick yourself? Or your customers?" Abeline asked.

He brushed that off. "It's a hoax. It's not real. The President says so, that the Chinese are trying to spread this thing all over the world, but that we can handle it."

"Handle what?"

"The virus, lady."

"The one you said was a hoax?"

He'd looked at Abeline like she was the dumbest human being left on Earth. "It's not as bad as they say, that's what I mean. The hoax part is the numbers. You've seen the film? The dead people lining the halls in China? Covered in sheets? Propaganda. They're all alive. Actors. This thing only kills old and sick people. You don't need those masks. I promise."

At two-eighteen in the morning, it felt very true to Slow Bear. The air in the empty lobby was just like the air everywhere else. Plus, it wasn't only his shoes he'd left upstairs, but his fucking mask, too.

The TV behind the front desk, still playing years-old basketball, was brutally loud. Slow Bear looked for a mask dispenser or stash of the damn things somewhere. The night manager was nowhere to be seen. The office door, closed. Unless he was asleep, he fucking well knew Slow Bear was out here. The camera was pointed right at him.

He could push the plastic buzzer, stuck on the counter with double-sided tape, but decided it wasn't worth talking to anyone else at the moment. He strolled down to the tiny breakfast room, only a few tables and mismatched chairs. There was no food out. Duh. What had he expected?

An orange juice with a foil lid you poke the straw through, like you get in the hospital, that would be nice. He was itching for orange juice. Sunkist was fine every now and then, but he really craved fresh-squeezed orange juice with heavy pulp. Like his noseless friend Hampton in Denver might say, "Aw, man, that's the good stuff."

But there wasn't a goddamn thing except a water dispenser with little paper cups. He downed a bunch of those. Lukewarm water. Air bubbles farted to the top as he filled cup after cup, drank them like shots. They *were* shots. Potent, clear, warmish shots. Yum.

The sign on the wall said breakfast was served from 6AM to 9:30AM. He didn't want to wait that long. Might as well bother the night manager about getting something sooner.

This time he did ring the bell. It made a muted bing-bong back in the office. No response.

Slow Bear heard rustling behind him. Someone sitting in one of the lobby chairs. A white man in jeans, scratched up Reeboks and a black button-up shirt. Hair slicked back like he'd just taken a shower. Another night owl, reading yesterday's paper in an empty hotel. Slow Bear had no idea where he'd come from. The elevator? Could be the TV drowned out the noise. Or maybe he was a ground floor guest?

Slow Bear inched around, hoping to get a look at the guy's face without catching his attention. Not sure why he was interested – some business traveler, insomniac, lunatic, who could tell? Whatever he was reading had him in deep. Oh, and he wasn't wearing a mask either. Another daredevil.

Man, that TV. When the game broke for commercials, Slow Bear thought he might as well be at a KISS concert. He stepped back to the desk, tried the button again. Couldn't hear the *bing-bong* this time over *Something something at your Buick dealer today!*

Still no response.

Fuck this. Slow Bear rounded the desk, looking for a remote control. There had to be one. He went through a few drawers, nothing. One was locked. He squatted, rifled through the shelves, booklets and papers and key cards and the manager's tobacco spit bottle and a used pair of latex gloves and so much other crap but no remote control.

Ask your doctor to prescribe Xlckevux today!

He got up. The computer screens were locked, a slideshow of photos of the hotel from different angles during sunnier times. He wished he know how to work the system, see how many people were actually staying here. The man in the lobby chair turned to the next page of his newspaper.

We're back to this thrilling exercise in futility between Fort Beehive and Plonk State–

Almost two-thirty. Slow Bear's ears were playing tricks on him. He yawned. Still wanted more to drink before heading back up. Abeline was right about him needing rest. His battery was hovering around twenty percent.

Funny. Here he was going through everything behind the desk and the manager hadn't noticed via the security camera? Definitely asleep.

So, Kemosabe, do you think Slow Bear should wake the guy up and ask if he can get some orange juice?

Either that or stand by the water cooler downing lukewarm shots until he quenched his thirst.

Orange juice won. It had taken the place of painkillers, booze and heroin in his life. Even coffee. Go too long without it, he got itchy.

Well, shit on a shingle, Doug, that was a sneaky play from the defense.

The office door was closed, the window plastered with announcements, schedules, and motivational sayings, giving whoever was working that shift their privacy. Slow Bear knocked. "Hey, guy. You up in there?" Another knock. "Rise and shine. Sorry about this."

Gave it thirty seconds.

Then knocked, like, twenty times in a row.

JE-sus-CHRIST!

He tried the door handle. "Knock, knock." It was open. He pushed the door, walked inside.

The night manager was in his chair, flopped forward onto the desk. His head smashed and scattered like a melon.

I bet this crowd didn't see THAT play coming, Conquistador!

Slow Bear's cop instinct kicked in, almost too late.

He reached back and kicked the office door shut just as the man from the lobby swung the sharp end of a hammer towards his head, smashing through the office window instead.

Slow Bear yanked the door inward, dragging the hammer and the attacker into the office off-balance. Slow Bear kicked him into the wall, then stomped on him a few times. The goon swung the hammer again, tapped Slow Bear's leg – just a sting.

An easy lay-up! Two points!

Slow Bear leapt over the goon's ass and back into the lobby, slamming into the wall under the TV. The goon righted himself and lifted the hammer again. Slow Bear skittled into the lobby and turned to face the guy.

Weapon, weapon, weapon. Who's got a weapon?

Why a fucking hammer? Why not a gun?

Less noise? Harder to trace?

The blaring TV covered a lot of sins.

FOUL!

The goon charged. If Slow Bear tried to run, the goon would catch up fast. No time. Slow Bear dropped to the floor in front of the guy like he was doing a push-up. The goon's shins slammed into Slow Bear's body, his knees bent back, and he tripped and skid across the lobby floor on his face.

Now Slow Bear hopped up and ran. Where to? Where to? Where to?

Cat scratch fever? Slather it in cream cheese. Only the best will do.

The breakfast room. He grabbed one of the mismatched chairs, wooden, and hefted it awkwardly in his hand.

Back out into the lobby where the goon was already rushing for him. Slow Bear swung the chair, bashed his attacker.

The goon got hold of the bottom leg of the chair, yanked it forward. His other hand stabbed the hammer.

Slow Bear kept the chair between them until the goon began twisting it. Slow Bear lost his grip.

Well, fuck me sideways, what a game!

He shoved all of his weight forward, sent the goon reeling.

Abeline's gun, up in the room. He'd left the Greek's Glock back in Denver. He'd tossed his stun gun back in the field with Gerardo. The fuck was he thinking?

He pinned the goon with the chair.

The goon tried to kick it off. No good.

Every kick sent aches rolling through Slow Bear. He needed another arm.

If I live a hundred more years, Doug, I don't think I'll ever see anything as pathetic as this.

The goon slapped the hammer around and finally smacked Slow Bear's hand with it.

Instinct. He let go of the chair and shook his hand. *"Goddamnit!"*

The goon kicked the chair into Slow Bear's face. A brilliant streak of pain. The chair fell and Slow Bear stumbled out of the way, his feet all twisted and turned, struggling to stay upright.

Neosporin antibiotic ointment, for the bad shit–

When he stopped spinning, the goon was behind him. *Swoosh.* Too late.

The back of the hammer sunk into his side. The goon ripped it out again. Aimed higher. Slow Bear grabbed the goon's arm. Held it straight up. Strained.

The goon kneed Slow Bear in the guts, once, twice. Fuck!

The goon clawed Slow Bear's eyes. Fuck! He spun off, squinting, flailing.

Thunk.

The hammer dug in again on Slow Bear's bad shoulder.

M o t h e r F U C K E R!

He opened his stinging eyes, still not more than a squint. The goon was in his face, loosening the hammer from Slow Bear's wound.

Slow Bear launched a *headbutt for the win!* Connected.

The goon went to his knees. The hammer slid out, still in the goon's hand.

Slow Bear ran for the front doors barefoot and bleeding.

How about something in Abeline's car? Like a tire tool.

But she'd locked the car. He remembered the beep.

Keys up in the room. Shit.

Outside, under the portico, Slow Bear hit the freezing wind, his feet ripped by the asphalt. Looked around. In addition to the hotel van – why the fuck did this shitty hotel have a van? – there were a few other cars besides Abeline's.

Only ten seconds left in this quarter. St. Plonk is getting massacred. Maybe try another car in the lot, maybe someone forgot to lock it. A buzzer beater! Will it go in? Trunk release. Tire tool.

If he could hurry, outrun the goon with the hammer long enough to try doors, hit the buttons, run around to the trunks… something that should only take seconds but he didn't have seconds because the sick fuck would whomp him in the skull with the hammer. So go go go *go go go.*

He took one running step and–

Smash!

Lucky the car just glanced Slow Bear's hip instead of clipping him dead center, but he still curled over the hood, slid off.

And that's the ball game, motherfucker!

A car he hadn't noticed. Black. Hidden in the dark away from the only bright pool of light over the hotel parking lot.

It kept on past Slow Bear and bashed a column, split it in two, fucked up the car's front end.

Slow Bear, on his back, tried to figure out if anything was broken. Hurt like a grudge fuck, but he was in one piece.

The car door opened. The driver unfurled. Shiny black loafers. Black slacks. A bad Christmas sweater three months too late. The barrel of a black pistol. A neck brace. A swollen jaw and bruised face.

Gerardo.

Rico fucking Suave indeed.

"Hey, look at this! You made it." Slow Bear rolled backwards onto his feet, into a crouch. Standing all the way up would hurt bad, he knew it would. "So, how are you doing?"

Worse, Gerardo might not let him stand up at all.

There was the barrel, rising.

One squeeze of the trigger.

But Gerardo froze.

The goon from inside came running out, hammer ready, but Gerardo waved him off.

What was he waiting for?

"You got nothing to say to me? Huh?"

Gerardo, his balloon face red and tight, leaned over, parted his lips, and showed Slow Bear a mouth full of steel wires.

Actually impressed Slow Bear. "Fuck. I did that?"

Gerardo slammed the gun into Slow Bear's skull.

CHAPTER 10

Smacking Slow Bear on the side of the head didn't knock him out.

It shook his brain. Concussion? Could be, could be. It sent a sudden lightning strike through his whole body, made him lurch forward on his hand and knees and throw up bile.

When there was nothing left, he dry heaved some more.

Both Gerardo and the goon stood over him.

He looked up.

Pistol in his face.

The goon slapped the hammer in his palm.

Slow Bear didn't have time for his life to pass before his eyes.

This was it.

Until the truck that serviced the vending machines bounced into the parking lot, lights blinding, speedy fucker. The driver braked hard short of the portico. Hispanic guy, company trucker hat, long arm hanging out the window, He leaned his head out. "Hey! What are you doing?"

Gerardo freaked and spun and fired at the truck. Slugs slamming, webbing the windshield, breaking through. The driver screamed, then sank in his seat.

Hotel guests spilled outside in jammies and winter coats, some in surgical masks, nearly all of them recording on their phones.

Slow Bear was way confused. Hurtin'.

He jumped up and grabbed the goon's hammer, slick with blood. The goon had a stiff grip on it and yelled for Gerardo to "*Shoot the bastard!*"

Slow Bear let out a bellow he didn't know he had in him and wrenched the hammer away from the goon. Fumbled it. Caught it again. Swung wildly at Gerardo. Got him in the arm, just enough to knock the gun out of line, the shot blinding, deafening, but headed up into the sky.

Slow Bear rushed Gerardo into the side of the car and pinned him, hammered away at his gun hand. Gerardo growled through his wired teeth, the bones in his fingers cracking to shards until the hand was a bag of splinters. The gun almost slipped out his grasp to the ground. Slow Bear caught it and shoved it into Gerardo's stomach, fired three times.

"Petey sends his love, asshole."

Then turned just as the goon was about to grab Slow Bear on both sides of his head. Slow Bear pulled the gun up and fired, the shot ripping through the goon's neck.

Surprised eyes. Quick, but it was there. Then he was dead weight.

One of the hotel guests – Slow Bear counted seven outside, looked past to see a few more in the lobby – was carrying, too. An old man, retired but with plenty of years left on the odometer, held a 1911 in both hands. "Hold up, son! Drop the gun!"

Fuck. He'd wanted to keep this one.

But now wasn't the time. Abeline, the girls?

He tossed the gun aside, held up his hands. "They attacked me! They killed the manager! I think they were trying to rob the place."

The old man wore thick metal-framed glasses, looked like he knew how to handle a gun. Thin white t-shirt, the cold not bothering him. Blue sweatpants and moccasin slippers.

"That's fine. Let's wait for the police and we'll figure it all out."

Slow Bear pointed. "My family's in there!"

"I'm sure they're okay. Everyone just calm down. Nine-one-one is on the way."

"I've got to go get them!"

Steady arm. "You're not going anywhere, boy."

More gunshots, muffled. *Bam bam bam*, from inside the hotel.

Oh shit.

Slow Bear took off. A painful, limping, determined sprint.

"Hey!"

The old man wasn't going to shoot. He was a peacemaker, not a killer. Fuck him.

Slow Bear ran for the stairwell, faster than the elevator. Hating himself on the climb back to his floor, unarmed *again*, a fool to think one goon was all he had to deal with. Then Gerardo fucked him up. So of course there had to be a third one, doing the deed while the other two dealt with Slow Bear. Reclaiming their property.

But three shots. Three girls.

He held hard to the rails, climbing as fast as he could but

goddamnitshitishitshit.

Maybe the fucker had used all three shots on Abeline, taking the girls unharmed. They were worth a lot of money.

The TV sports announcer's voice in his head again: *Hurry. This is overtime!*

Fourth floor door. He opened it and lurched into the hallway, not giving a shit for his own safety anymore. Let them shoot. Let them carve his skin. He'd only die when he knew what happened to his girls.

His girls.

Known them a day and that's how he thought of them.

He had a feeling in his chest like the night Kylie was stolen. A taste in his mouth like piss and vinegar. Running for the room on the other side of the building. A couple of hotel guests peeked out their doors as he passed.

Finally, the room.

The door, wide open.

Dark inside. He rounded the door into the room and–

Another gunshot.

The closet door beside his head splintered.

He flinched and dropped. Too close. He waited for the next one. The last one.

"Micah! For fuck's sake, Micah!"

He looked up. Blinked.

Abeline, two-fisting her revolver, standing there in her t-shirt and boxers. The girls knelt beside her on the far side of the second bed against the wall, peeking over the side.

Sprawled between the two beds, face down, another goon. Gun in his hand – *all these guns, for fuck's sake* – but two exit wounds on his back.

CHAPTER 11

Slow Bear checked the goon. Yep, dead. Blood and gore splattered on the walls.

"Everyone good, right?"

"Jesus, Micah!"

He leaned over towards the girls. "You both okay? Didn't get hurt?"

Melody wheezed. Pia said, "Miss Abeline knew what to do."

"Good. Good."

"What's going on?"

"Yeah," Abeline said. "Where did you go? Why weren't you here? We could've been killed!"

Then she got a load of how he'd fared.

"Oh my God!" Reached for the wound on his shoulder. Then slid her hand down to the other gouge on his side. "Look at you!"

"No time. We've got to go, fast. Grab the bags. Get your keys."

"You need help."

"No time, I said. Come on, come on!"

"Can't we–"

"*No. Time.* There's a man with a gun down there, already called the cops. There's two other men could've killed me. Almost did. We don't want to fuck with the cops right now."

He grabbed the Target bags, his wallet, ran out of space in his hand.

Abeline shook her head. "I don't... I... the cops can help the girls. You need an ambulance."

"I'd go to jail, and the girls will go into the system."

"I'll take them! They can stay with me!"

"That's not how it works! Just, Jesus, shut up and follow me."

She shook herself out of her post-kill stupor, gave Slow Bear a grizzly look. "Come on, girls. Let's go. Follow this idiot."

He pushed them into the hall. Abeline dodged him and reached back for her purse, on top of the minifridge.

"Hold up." Slow Bear turned around. He had to drop the Target bags so he could pry the goon's gun out of his not-yet-cold dead hand.

"Keeping this one."

Back to the hall. The door shut behind him. They high-tailed it to the stairwell.

Out the exit on the ground floor, the far side of the hotel, around the corner from the front lot where all the action was. It was freezing, none of them dressed for it. Melody couldn't help but whine, "*Coooold. It's so cold it hurts! Miss Abeline!*"

She knelt beside the girls and tried to quiet them while Slow Bear snuck to the corner and took a look at the scene he'd left only a few minutes earlier. A sole Sheriff's SUV had shown up, with only one deputy. There would be more, though. Plenty more and soon. The guests shouted and pointed, some at Gerardo's car and body, some at the lobby, some up in the sky.

Abeline's car was too close to the crowd, too out in the open. Waiting for the crowd to leave would take forever. The girls would be popsicles by then.

F-*f-f-f*uck. The cold was getting to him, too.

If they could make it to the vendor's truck, push him out of the driver's seat. It would give them all something to eat, too.

No time, no time.

The deputy held his arms wide, guiding everyone back to the lobby like a flock of swans. Slow Bear tried to get a better view – where was the old man with the gun? How many were left? Had they found the night manager's body yet? But his view was blocked by the hotel van, the one covered in dust with low tires, parked almost flush to the hotel wall.

Goddamn van.

Lightbulb.

Glorious van!

He turned to Abeline, motioned for her to stay put.

She hunched her shoulders. *What the fuck are you talking about?*

Whatever.

Slow Bear crouched, started waddling towards the side of the van closest to the wall. Not a lot of room, but as long as he could reach the van's sliding side door and open it, he could help the girls and Abeline inside.

At the back bumper. The space was even thinner than it had looked at first. His legs were starting to hurt, his feet numb, his fingers aching. Turn around? Look for another way out of here? If it was just him, or just him and Abeline…

He sat on the asphalt, jagged gravel and broken glass biting into him. He scooted along the side of the van. Steel in his face, stucco at his back, squeezing the air out of his lungs. It's not like he was a thick man. Slow Bear didn't eat as much as he should, pretty lean with a fast metabolism. Still, this van was kicking his ass.

He had to sneeze. Tried to hold it. Kept holding.

It came out like a bark.

Two, three times.

He held his breath, tried to see if anyone might've heard him.

Footsteps crunching.

It had been a good run, but he'd never find Kylie now, nor the shitbag who'd bought the girls so Slow Bear could make him suffer in his last minutes on the planet.

Instead, he was going straight to jail. Multiple murders. He'd left a trail of destruction across the plains, up into the mountains, getting a lot farther along on fumes and luck than he'd thought possible.

Goddamn it, he didn't want to stop now.

He wouldn't last in prison. There were more than enough prices on his head. More than enough contracts on his life. Most likely, day one in prison, he'd be torn limb from limb – finishing what the shotgun had started on his arm. They would rip him to pieces, then fuck all the pieces. They would keep Slow Bear alive long enough to watch it happen, then cut his head from his neck and have someone fuck his throat, too.

That's only if he even made it out of this parking lot alive. Indians made good target practice for white cops. He should know. As a rez cop, he'd worked with plenty of white cops who would've loved an excuse to shoot him.

Footsteps, closer. Crunching. Chirpy muffled voices on the deputy's radio. String of numbers. *Chirp*. Unintelligible. *Chirp*.

Flashlight beam, coming through the windshield. Quick hits, this way and that.

Chirp. "Could've sworn I heard…" *Chirp*.

Footsteps along the opposite side of the van. He was coming around.

This was best for Abeline and the girls, though. They'd get taken care of. Warm beds, warm food. Coffee. They would tell the authorities what happened. They would be *safe*.

For a little while.

The girls would end up in the system, separated, moved to group homes and foster homes, maybe exploited, maybe forced into hardcore religion, maybe left to drift wayward. Not as awful as what was waiting for them in California, but still, it was no life for these kids.

Abeline? A target on her back? A witness in court? Jailtime? Or maybe she'd go right back to her lonely small-town life. Maybe she'd pick up a string of one-night stands, none of them as interesting as Slow Bear, to keep her company. Maybe one of those, you never know, might end up being a comfort to her for a lot longer than a couple nights.

Either way, it had to beat freezing her ass to death in a run-down hotel parking lot.

Chirp.

CHAPTER 12

Headlights cut across the deputy, the whole parking lot. Strobing cop lights. Two more sheriff's vehicles – a squad and a raised pick-up.

The deputy said, "About fucking time" and took off to meet them.

Slow Bear let out a ragged breath. Clunked his head back against the stucco wall and stared straight up at the sliver of dark night sky.

The closest thing to a prayer he'd ever thought: *Thank fuck.*

Then he reached for the side door handle for the van.

Well, what do you know? Damn thing was unlocked.

Another quick prayer as he slowly slid it open: *Now you're just fucking with me, aren't you?*

Slow Bear looked back and waved them over, still trying to keep an eye and ear on the deputy, hoping he'd forgotten all about the noise he thought he'd heard.

Abeline sent the girls one at a time, Melody first. She ran straight for Slow Bear, easily fit in the narrow space by the van, and Slow Bear lifted her inside. Then Pia, who didn't run. Much more aware, much more cautious. No problem for her fitting through.

Abeline was last. Halfway down the wall, Slow Bear thought he heard cop voices coming back. More *chirps* from their radio handsets.

"Same guy they're looking for in Denver."

"Really?"

"You didn't hear about that? Total massacre at a Carl's Jr. Bloodbath. And it's got to be the same guy. A one-armed Indian."

Shit. Abeline was in No Man's Land, a deer on alert, both hands strangling her purse strap.

Slow Bear got her attention. *Keep coming.*

She shook her head.

Get over here now.

I can't!

Faces and hands conveying it all.

Second cop voice, "I almost threw up when I saw the manager. Oh, god, the fuck was that all about?"

"Meat's off the menu for a few days. Or anything red. Just make that anything red."

Slow Bear gave Abeline his hardest look: *Get your ass over here RIGHT NOW or I swear...*

Abeline rushed ahead, had a little bit of trouble sliding along, but Slow Bear reached for her the last couple of inches, pulled her by the waist and shoved her into the van, the girls pitching in to help catch her without any noise.

Slow Bear was still out on the ground. He put a finger to his lips. The girls huddled around Abeline, trying to keep their teeth from chattering, as the cops swept past the van.

"What about the other guys? The guy with the neck brace?"

"Jesus. I almost don't want to know. No ID. His jaw's wired shut."

They walked around the corner of the building.

"Want to check the stairs, or…"

Sigh. "I don't know, man. Weird shit happening inside."

"You scared?"

"Fuck you."

"I'll go."

"Just… wait a bit, man. Let's get some coffee."

"Yeah, fine. I've got to hit the head anyway."

They turned. Slow Bear felt the flashlight stab him in the eyes, no way they could miss him now. But they kept up their cop bullshit and walked on by. The van? Invisible to them.

"Poor guy, that delivery driver. Goddamn."

"Adios, Pedro."

They laughed and laughed. Walked towards the hotel entrance.

Slow Bear ached all over. Numb fingers, numb toes. Throbbing hammer wounds. A headache stampeding across his skull.

Abeline grabbed his arm, tried to help him up, but struggled. Pia reached out, caught him by the t-shirt. It started to slip over his head. "No no no no no."

"I'm sorry!"

"Don't say anything. Just, let go."

She did. Then he was free, but it pained him to stand. His back, fuck, his back. Abeline pulled him into the van. Pia started to slide the door shut, but Slow Bear said, "Wait!"

Too late. It slammed and clicked into place.

They all went dead still. Waiting for the cops to double back.

Breath hung in the air, slowly fading.

No one came.

The van had two captain's chairs and three bench seats, typical shuttle bus. It had seen better days – ripped seats now, sticky floor. They huddled together on the middle bench. The girls' shivering like jackhammers, Abeline trying her best to keep them warm next to her body.

"Now what?"

Slow Bear look around. He rubbed his leg with his hand, looked at his palm. It was too dark to see blood, but he knew it was there. "I don't know."

"Jesus, what do you mean–"

"We need to get to your car."

"My car? I don't have my keys. I left them in the room."

"They're not in your purse?"

"I tossed them on the table. I always those them on the table. Even at home, I toss them on the table."

"Seriously? I told you–"

"I shot a man!" *Hisssss.*

"So did I! But the keys!"

"What about all the clothes we bought? I thought you got those. We're freezing!"

"I had to drop them to get the guy's gun!"

"You chose a *gun* over our *clothes*?"

"I needed it!"

Louder: "Oh, Fuck you, Micah."

"Language!"

"No. No *language*. The girls need to learn. Girls, when a man lets you down, you tell him, 'Fuck you!'"

"Fuck you," Melody said. Abeline squeezed her closer.

"Yeah," Pia said, her arms crossed low across her stomach. "Fuck you. I don't feel so good."

Slow Bear looked around. A thin ray of parking lot light wasn't enough to let him make out details in the van. No blankets, no jackets, nothing. No keys to turn the heater on. Not a chance of sneaking back to the room.

The room.

How long before the cops found the body up there? How long before they linked that room to Abeline's car in the parking lot? And how long before someone said, *Maybe we should check that van over there*?

What a failure. A fucking failure. If there was a chance he could let Abeline and the girls escape while turning himself in, he would do it. Yes sir, he would. But every "Choose Your Own Adventure" path he took in his head turned bad. Real bad. Bullet-ridden bad. Abeline-charged-with-murder bad. Girls-worse-than-where-they-started bad.

Catch in his throat. In spite of the pain from his wounds, the pressure in his chest for being exposed as a fraud felt ten times worse.

Slow Bear turned back to them, lowered his eyes. "I'm sorry, guys."

Abeline rubbed her cheek against the top of Pia's head. "It's fine."

They all huddled close in the dark.

CHAPTER 13

Slow Bear couldn't sleep. Of course not. He felt himself on the verge of passing out, just like Abeline and the girls were doing – nodding off, jerking awake.

He took in a big breath through his nose. He had to stay awake this time. Stay aware.

There was slightest hint of gray morning sky. Or that could've been Slow Bear's eyes playing tricks on him. The inside of the van seemed brighter by a fraction. If he looked at the back of the captain's chairs, the dash console between them, it was as if they were made of white noise. Old-fashioned TV fuzz. Every one of his blinks was a micro-nap. A reboot that never made it through the full cycle.

He tried to shake it off. Tried to keep from going under.

More cop cruisers. Another ambulance. Strobing lights fading as the sun rose.

He needed to do something, anything, *something*. He was no sitting duck, even if he had caught one in the wing once.

He eased himself out from under Melody's head on his chest, Abeline's legs twisted up with his, and crept from the bench. Careful, not wanting to attract attention if there was still anyone around, but it looked like the police and EMTs had retreated inside, into the warmth, leaving the bodies out front, no sheet, no one keeping an eye over them.

Something funky was lodged in his throat. He tried to clear it without waking the others. Not fucking likely, so he tried to choke it down. Like swallowing sandpaper.

Think, asshole, think.

The only play was to head up to the room via the back stairs. He'd closed the door behind him, so maybe it would still be awhile before the cops figured it out. What did they have to work with, anyway?

Security cameras.

Other guests.

A very long trail of his own blood from the lobby, up the stairs, to the room, then back down again.

Stupid blood, bleeding like that.

Still, it was the only way.

He picked up the gun he'd taken from the goon, then thought better of it. Put it down. He did not want to get caught by cops carrying that thing.

Indian with a gun + any cop ever = dead Indian.

What else?

He checked out the console between the front seats. Spare nickels stuck in place by soda pop circles. Nail clippers. Half-a-pack of spearmint gum. Some ashes that probably weren't supposed to be there.

He looked into the glove compartment. Okay. Some paperwork. A tire gauge. Couple of folded maps, courtesy of whatever chain this hotel used to be. A bottle of bubbly water, cherry-flavored, and a power bar. Granola-honey-raisins, maybe. He couldn't read the wrapper in this light. So hungry he almost ripped it open right then and there, but remembered he should probably let the girls and Abeline split it.

None of that was going to help him get back upstairs.

The sun visors. The one over the driver's seat looked wonky. The other one was right like it was supposed to be, tight against the ceiling. But the other one looked broken, not flush.

There is absolutely no way they are that stupid–

He reached for the visor, pulled it down.

A set of keys fell into the chair.

Whispered, "No way."

You just watched it happen.

Slow Bear's luck usually ran between none and in the red. Maybe for once–

Another cop cruiser took the curb hard and bounced into the parking lot, skidded to a stop over Gerardo's body. Front tire rolled right over the fucker's hand.

Slow Bear ducked. Watched the cops get out, laughing, as another one came out of the hotel, all, "*Hey, you almost ran over my victim!*"

"Poor guy's had a bad night."

All three headed into the hotel lobby.

Slow Bear let out a breath he didn't know he was holding. He picked up the keys from the seat. The one for the van was marked, the others looked like old-fashioned room keys before everyone switched to cards. How long since this van had been used?

Anyway.

Slow Bear slid into the driver's seat. Wished he knew some sort of mystical shit to appease the gods or whatever. He slid the key into the slot and…

Nothing.

Well, if at first you don't succeed.

Again.

This time, the engine woke up and coughed. Loudly.

The belts squealed.

The damned van shook all over.

From behind him, "Dear Lord!"

Slow Bear looked over his shoulder. Abeline was awake, startled, trying to get her bearings.

They both waited, because there was no way this tin can wasn't going to attract attention.

Abeline slipped from between the still-sleeping girls and moved to the next bench up. She reached out and gripped Slow Bear's shoulder.

Wasn't one soul coming to check on them.

"You okay with leaving her?" He chinned towards her car ahead of them in the lot.

"Piece of shit. I needed to get rid of it anyway."

"When they find you later, tell them it was stolen. Tell them everything was stolen."

He one-eightied the van, hopped the back curb, and slid away across the mostly empty wilderness, nobody chasing them.

CHAPTER 14

Warmth. That was the priority.

Slow Bear had the heat on high in the van. He was sweating like a bastard, the vents like a blast furnace.

On he drove. They'd come out of the forest by a combo taco-and-fish place. Or chicken-and-burgers. It was hard to tell. The sign out front said NOW SERVING BREAKFAST/DRIVE-THRU ONLY.

That ghost town feeling he'd had before was doubled here, a strip of off-interstate gas stations, fast food, and adult bookstores. Too early in the morning for a couple of those joints to be doing business, but the others, it was like the Rapture.

Where the hell was everyone?

He didn't know if this was good or bad for him – good because there were fewer people to pay any attention to them, bad because no traffic made the stolen white hotel van stick out like an infected cyst.

Luckily, there was always a truck stop close-by, brightly-lit, wide-open, doing plenty of business. Abeline ducked inside to buy some new clothes – again – and some breakfast, but not before first having to double back for a mask. "They said no mask, no service."

While she was inside, Pia woke up. She climbed into the empty captain's chair without asking. Was she supposed to ask? Why should she? Slow Bear felt like he was supposed to scold her, but didn't want to. He would have to follow Abeline's lead on how to treat the girls. Melody was laid out on the bench, snoring. Pia sat with her legs folded beneath her, arms crossed like she was cold, but the heat was still on nuclear. To Slow Bear, anyway. How come he was pouring sweat, and his throat was so dry, and his head felt like the drums from a Slayer tune? Pia looked like it wasn't bothering her at all.

"How you doing, kid?" More like a croak.

She shrugged. "I'm sorry you got so beat up."

"That's what the other guy said." Wink.

She grinned. "I'm so sorry. All about us, too. I'm so sorry we got you into this. But thanks. I haven't said thanks."

"Don't thank me yet."

"You know, if you want to drop us off at a hospital or something, I'd understand. If we're too much trouble."

He shook his head, which turned up the drums. "You're no trouble. We're going to get you someplace safe. Do you have other family? Like an aunt or something?"

"Pretty sure my aunt gave my mom the idea about pimping me in the first place. I don't know about Melody. The man already had her when he got me."

"Cousins? Grandmas?"

She stared out the windshield. "My meemaw had me for awhile, me and my brother. He's ten years older than me. He fought with Meemaw all the time. He stole her wine money, and she hit him with a fireplace poker a lot. He left as soon as he could."

"Jesus."

What sort of soap opera was this? The kid ever had a normal day in her life? Seemed the best thing that happened to her was meeting Slow Bear – killer, bent cop, cripple, broke, pissed off, and taking advantage of a nice older lady to go look for a woman he didn't even love. But since Kylie getting swiped was his fault, he owed it to her to make a go of it.

The fuck was he going to do with these two girls? Carry them around like Baby Yodas?

"Hey," he tilted his chin up. "You sure you're pregnant?"

Her face went red. She wouldn't look at him. "I took a test. They made me take a test."

"What happened? They didn't use protection? You know, a condom? Or a pill?" *Why am I asking her this? What does it matter?* "Forget it. Never mind."

"They didn't know." She ran a finger around the edge of the glove compartment. "He told me his name was Morpheus. It was weird. Anyway, he was nice to me. He was supposed to drive me from place to place. That's it, just drive, and wait in the living room until we were done. I don't know. He was nice. All the others said I was pretty, but he was really nice." Shifty shoulders. She crossed her arms again. "When's Miss Abeline coming back?"

"A few minutes. Getting you some breakfast."

"I'm cold."

"Sorry. I'm boiling."

She narrowed her eyes at him. "You don't look so good. You're wet."

The sweat was a fucking waterfall. He pressed his palm to his head. Burning up. He would need to send Abeline back inside for Advil. No, some NyQuil. He needed a long nap. He looked at his palm. Dried blood had turned into a dripping mess.

"Tell, me, Pia." He cleared his throat. "Where is he now? The father? Morpheus? Do you think he'd help if we called him?"

There was a catch in her breath. "After they made me take the test, you know, the pee test? They were really mad at me. Really mad. But they told him not to worry about it. They told him he'd be assigned to a new girl. They told him they'd give him a raise. He wanted to talk to me, I know, he was shouting from the other room. Shouting my name. But then he left, and then they put me in a car."

Figures. Morpheus, whatever his name was, was dead. Sure as shit, he had to be. Maybe after he found Kylie, he'd go check into this guy some more.

No he wouldn't. Stupid. Thinking like that was what got him here in the first place.

The side of the van slid open, and Abeline was out there with two bulging bags. She'd pulled sweatpants and a sweatshirt – "Colorado" swept across the front – over her t-shirt and boxers. Still barefoot. A greasy paper bag was tucked under her arm.

Pulled her mask under her chin. "Sweats for every one! Hope that's okay. Got some biscuits. Sausage and cheese. And some chocolate milk."

Pretty cheery considering what they'd just gone through. She was making do. The horror of it could settle later. Right now, Slow Bear could tell Abeline was committed to these girls. Bet she was a good mom, a good grandma. A good wife, even. Fucked over by crap men.

Must've been the fever getting to him. No one was *that* good. She had her secrets, had to have. Like shouting slurs while she rode his cock. Racist bitch.

Pia climbed back and took the paper bag, dug out a biscuit. Melody, still half-asleep, sat up and yawned about as loud as she'd been snoring. Stretched her arms high.

Abeline handed the girls their new sweats, then finally looked over at Slow Bear and her face collapsed. "Holy shit."

She looked all around her, then climbed in, slid the door closed behind her. Knelt beside Slow Bear.

"Good god, Micah, you look dead already."

Pressed her fingers to his head, then hers, then his again. "Oh no. Oh no, oh no, oh no."

He said, "Advil."

"Sweetie, let me drive."

He caught a glimpse of himself in the rearview mirror. Thought he was shaking his head no at her, but he wasn't moving at all. He was pale as paste with purple shadows.

"Baby, my lord, I think we need to take you to the hospital."

"No, no, please. No hospital. You can… you can drive. Hand me a biscuit."

Then he passed out.

CHAPTER 15

There she was. Kylie, wiping down the bar in the casino where she used to work. Where Slow Bear had met her and spent most of his post-arm waking days. Where he'd fallen for her, called her "Lady," but never made a move because, well, she deserved better. She was a decade-plus younger than him. Last thing she needed in her life was his avalanche of bullshit, and yet, she somehow got roped into driving him to Williston, ferrying him around town to help him fulfill his promise to his former boss, and sleeping in the car beside him in a WalMart parking lot. Where they'd taken her from him. Where they'd nearly stomped his head into goo.

The casino now looked like it had before all that, when things were still okay if not good. It was too good to be true. Must've been a dream.

But hey, this felt real.

Kylie, in one of her tight spandex tank-tops, D-cups full of baby fat spilling out. She was a thick girl, yes she was. Hair pulled back into a tail. Just the lightest bit of make-up, lip gloss. The closer he walked, the stronger her smell – Dove soap and apple shampoo. She looked up at him. She smiled.

Slow Bear looked left, then right. No gamblers. No pit bosses. No dealers. Nobody at all. The machines were still clanging, bleeping and blooping. He had goosebumps. Bright lights, stinging his eyes.

As he settled on his usual barstool – the only one this time – Lady already had a glass of fresh-squeezed orange juice ready for him. Any other time, it would've been a beer, one he'd nurse until it was warm. He hated the taste.

"Thank you." He picked up his orange juice. Plenty of pulp.

"My life is Hell," she said.

The juice went sour in his mouth, like he'd just brushed his teeth. He spat it all over the bar. Kylie wiped it up as if nothing happened.

"I am raped every day. More than once. All the time. I'm fucking raped all the fucking time. Do you understand? All the time."

He wiped his mouth with the back of his hand. A hand that shouldn't be there. He lifted two arms, stared at two hands. How did this happen?

"I'm sorry, I'm so sorry. I've never given up, though. I'm going to find you. I swear."

She kept wiping. "Got me hooked on scag. I'll fuck anything for more of that shit. I'm sick all the time. I never get enough. You see me? You see how I look? I don't look like this anymore. I've lost weight. I'm losing my hair. I'm bruised all over. I've scratched my skin so bad it's infected."

"I'm sorry."

"Doesn't matter, though. They put me in a short dress and paint my face and lips and send me on to the next one. Raped. You name it, mouth, vagina, ass, they rape it."

Slow Bear stood and braced both – *both* – arms on the bar. Sweating again. "I said I'm sorry. What do you want me to do? I'm trying as hard as I can, goddamn it!"

Kylie kept wiping. "Oh, so now you're mad at me for getting kidnapped? For being raped most of my day? You're mad because you couldn't save me?"

"I'm trying, I said. Shit, that motherfucker Santana killed me once already. A hot shot of heroin." Luckily, one of the girls at the Mile High Club had a shot of Narcan to bring him back. "I shouldn't even be alive."

"Good to hear. Did I mention the rape?"

Slow Bear reached for the glass of orange juice, ready to sling it at the nearest incessant flashing one-armed bandit. But when he wound up and let go, he spun in circles and nothing smashed against anything.

He looked back at the bar. Glass was still there.

He looked down. His arm was gone.

His eyes snapped open.

Flat on his back on the last bench of the van, the road jolting him. He sucked in a big breath of air like he was coming up from a deep dive, sucked paper mask into his mouth. Then he started coughing, man, oh fuck, the sort of cough that sounded like and felt like bones cracking.

Above him, looking down in a mask way too big for her face, hanging like a feedbag, was Melody.

"Hey."

She was in stereo.

Then she turned and shouted, "Miss Abeline! He's alive!"

"What did I tell you about going back there, girl? Get up here, now! Hurry!"

Ringing in Slow Bear's ears.

"He's alive, I said!"

"Of course he's alive, sweetie. Get up here!"

"Go on, kid." Surprised by how weak his voice was. "Listen to her."

"I'm glad you're not dead, Micah."

"Go on, kid."

She scrambled off the bench and ran away.

Another bumpy stretch of highway. Felt like he was on the rack. He started to take a deep breath, but it was like sucking syrup through a straw. Fuck's sake! Took all his upper body strength to get half a lungful. Let it out with a "*Mutt-er-fuck*" and worried he'd never get more back again. He'd had his hide kicked plenty of times, but the shit that went down in that hotel might've been the baseball bat that broke the camel's back. Pretty sure he was dying.

But I've been dying for a couple years now.

Lost his arm. Lost his job. Lost his way. Lost Kylie. Lost his trailer. Lost his grip on the wagon. Lost his fucking mind ever since – one way ticket to Hell.

Another breath. Ho. Lee. Shit. Tug-o-war, man.

The van slowed. He braced himself to keep from sliding off the bench. The whole world spun as Abeline exited the interstate. He had forgotten where they were. He'd almost forgotten his own name and who the hell Abeline was. Another few swinging turns – Slow Bear queasy – and the van came to a stop. Slow Bear's ass was numb. He looked down. Had on a new Colorado sweatshirt and sweatpants. The woman had dressed him while he was unconscious. She'd even pinned his empty sleeve.

Door opened. Door closed. Door slid open. "Now, girls, stay right outside here. Don't go anywhere. Right outside the door where I can see you."

"Can we take our masks off?"

"For just a minute, and turn away from the van."

"Can we have a Mountain Dew?"

"Do what I said."

Blink. Blink.

There was a face in the dark. A face Slow Bear hadn't seen in a long goddamn time.

Blink.

Fat man. Missing a foot. "Finally got something in common, boy."

Wasn't real. Wasn't really there.

Blink. Blink.

"Scoot over." Abeline's voice. Abeline! His knees knocked together as she sat on the bench beside him. Now it was her face, half-covered with a mask. Sad eyes. Crow's feet. She reached out, felt his forehead, shook her head. "Still hot, still really hot."

Blink.

"Abeline? You doing okay?"

"Better than you."

"I've had worse."

"Have you? You think? I've been listening to the radio. This virus is called COVID, they said."

"A flu?"

"Not a flu. Not a cold. Not sure what it is. They said it comes from bats."

"Bats?"

"People in China eating bats, and now we've got it, too."

Slow Bear started to laugh, then coughed. Then coughed so hard his brain shut down for a moment and he saw that fat man's face again, spitting off to the side. "You don't even know if I'm alive or dead, boy. You haven't bothered to check in a long time, have you?"

His own papaw – his mom's dad, the only grandparent he knew – sitting outside on the front porch of a house too fancy for him, belonging to his daughter, Slow Bear's older sister, who'd taken him in. So he heard. He'd never been to his sister's house. His brain was just doing some guessing, he supposed.

His sister's name was Heather.

Thinking this while his vision went blinding white and he couldn't catch his breath, Abeline telling him, "It's alright, it's alright, breathe, baby, breathe for me."

He finally got a breath, surprised he didn't drown. Felt as if his lungs were full of seawater. "Oh, *God help me.*"

"Hush, now, it's okay. It's okay." But the way she said it sounded like it wasn't okay at all.

Melody's voice shouting from outside, "Miss Abeline, Pia's looking at you inside the van and she doesn't have her mask on!"

"Shut up, narc!"

"Don't call me that!"

"Shut the shit up!"

Abeline whipped around. "Please, quiet, both of you."

Pia said, "Is he going to be okay?"

"We'll see. You have to let him rest. He needs some quiet."

"Are *we* going to be okay?"

Slow Bear expected her to say, *Of course we will. It's just a flu. We're all going to be peachy.*

Instead, "I don't know, hon. Hope and pray, that's all we can do. Hope and pray."

Slow Bear fought to sit up. Abeline helped. "Water?"

She unscrewed one of the green glass bottles, gave it to him. He took a little sip. Swallowing was a nightmare, but he was thirsty. He swallowed some more. Regretted it.

"Where are we?"

"Right inside the Utah state line."

"Utah?"

"That's what I said."

"Why did you keep going? Dump me on the side of the road and get these girls some help."

"Jesus, you sure are a martyr, ain't you?"

"I'm worthless, leave me behind."

"Out of your goddamned mind."

Slow Bear put down the water, reached for his mask, piece of shit thing, but Abeline held his hand down. "Look, now, let me sleep this off in a men's room stall, and you go on. I'll make my own way to Salt Lake City, and you guys can be far away from here."

Abeline lifted her chin. Old lady neck. "God almighty, baby. That's your plan now? Back in Denver, it was fine parking the girls half a block from the assholes, but now you're worried?"

"That was then. It's just, are you listening? It's just going to get worse from here. Cops are looking for me, looking for the van. You guys ought to go find a car for sale in someone's yard, pay cash, and get gone."

"You're trying to get rid of me."

"Oh god, you stupid bitch."

"Stupid bitch is saving your life, you piece of shit. I'm not leaving you anywhere until I say so. Right now, we either get you better or get you to a hospital. Are you going to help me or feel sorry for yourself?"

Slow Bear fell back on the bench. Holding himself up had sapped his strength and then some. That Abeline, though. Tough woman. Glad she'd decided to take him home that night. Maybe she wasn't as hot as some others he'd fucked along the way, but she was still pretty damn warm, and definitely warmer than *most* of the one-night stands. At least she didn't have pimples on her ass. How many others would've invited the girls in for Pop-Tarts, even?

Right on cue, there was Pia standing behind Abeline's shoulder, wide-eyed at his condition.

"Okay, okay. Find us a campground. Like, you know, a park or something. One for RVs. Hide us back in the trees. They'll leave us alone."

"A campground? Like a tent?"

"The van will do."

"Out. Of. Your. Mind. How am I supposed to start a fire? What about food? How am I supposed to take care of the girls–"

Slow Bear tried to mumble, "Whatever," but couldn't be sure it crossed his lips before he blacked out again.

There was his papaw, waiting for him. "Is she robbing the cradle, or are you robbing the nursing home?" Then he laughed and laughed and laughed.

CHAPTER 16

Just like the casino in Slow Bear's fever-addled mind, the neighborhood around Heather's house back on the rez was empty. No traffic, no kids, no hip-hop blaring from the windows. On the front porch, Slow Bear sat on a swing, two-armed again, while his papaw, half-Indian, half-bison, spilled over what had once been a kitchen chair and table. On the table now – ashtray, full, couple of cans of Coca-Cola, dregs. Tiny bottles of Sailor Jerry's rum his friends snuck him under Heather's nose.

He said, "Even my drinking problem has a sweet tooth."

The old man didn't wear a prosthetic for his missing foot. He'd learned to walk on the stump, got used to the pain. Had a callous thick as a rubber sole, almost as black. He poured another bottle of rum into his sweating glass of Coke.

"Papaw?"

"So which is it? Alive or dead?"

"Alive."

"Good guess."

"Well, are you?"

"How the hell should I know? I do know you, son, are fucked." He laughed. Oh boy, did he laugh. "Not like either one of us would be called healthy. But you, goddamn, you got this virus."

"It's a flu."

"It is *not* a flu. It is like drowning on dry land. Your lungs fill up with gloopy shit. It fucks with your heart. It steals all your mojo. When it's done with you, it kills you."

"Jesus." Slow Bear looked down at his arms, his legs, the rest of him. Not aching at the moment. Not gasping at the moment. "Jesus."

Papaw stared out across the street. His eyes were almost slits because his fat cheeks pushed his lids closed. Slow Bear had never seen his eyes fully open.

He'd spent a lot of time with his grandfather on the rez when he was younger. His old house was different from this one, and there was no front porch. Just a dirt patch and folding chairs, an old tree stump turned into a table. An extension cord running to a boom box. Papaw loved Big-Ass Seventies rock bands – ZZ Top and April Wine. He started drinking every morning at six a.m. – rum in his coffee. Must've gone through a couple of gallons or more of rum, beer, and cheap red wine every day, but Slow Bear had never seen the man at anything other than even keel. Alcohol for him was like gas for a tractor.

Slow Bear felt like a ten-year-old around him again. Papaw was funny, and he gave Slow Bear sips of rum and beer and he smoked long brown cigarettes that he lit with one of about twenty plastic lighters out front and all over his house. A real fire hazard if you had a young, curious boy around.

He lit one now, even though Slow Bear had heard Papaw stopped smoking several years ago after surviving throat cancer, his neck a patchwork of scars. "So tell me, boy, what's new?"

Slow Bear shrugged. "I don't know."

"You don't know? Then who the hell else does?"

"I mean, I think I got myself good and lost."

Smoke rolled out Papaw's nose, mouth, ears, and neck scars. "Sounds about right."

"If I want to find Kylie, then I have to follow… I mean, I have to… if I follow the… shit. I have no idea what I'm doing. Now I got this woman and these girls in the middle of it, and I can't even protect them. I didn't sign up to protect anybody anyway."

"Thought you were a cop once. Protect and serve? That's what you're doing now. Protecting and serving. Otherwise, these girls end up in a pervert's fuck dungeon, and the old lady dropped in a hole in the desert."

"I can't save everyone. I can't even save one person."

"Goddamn." Papaw coughed and coughed. Hacked up a lung. "I'm bored. I'm bored talking to you about this."

"Wait, what?" Slow Bear looked down. Back to one arm. He looked up at his grandfather again. "What?"

"I just figured this out, son. Look at you, using some fever dream as an excuse to take yourself off the hook. It's boring as fuck. We're not gonna do this. How about I give you a fiver, you run down to the store, get me some cigarettes and some more of these little Sailor Jerry's?"

He took the fiver. Man, he really did feel like a kid again. He got up, started off the porch. He turned back to his papaw, staring across the street again, smoke still leaking from all his holes.

Down the sidewalk. Swirling fog. Slow Bear knew he'd never make it to the store.

Whatever this dream or vision was, whatever. Was it supposed to help? It didn't. It didn't do a damned thing except confuse him.

The fog swirled closer.

Wait, what had he been thinking about?

Closer still.

Where was he, anyway?

CHAPTER 17

"Hey, wake up."

It was Abeline, scooting his legs aside again.

"Some more NyQuil. Some water."

He sat up without opening his eyes. Too much strain to do two things at once. Pretty sure he'd been dreaming, but it had disappeared, except for the sickly sweet taste of rum in his mouth. When he opened his eyes, Abeline handed him a little cup filled with green medicine. Still wearing her mask. Of course, why wouldn't she?

He blinked, dim light outside, trees nearby on all sides. "Where… is this?"

"Campground. State park. Cheap and nobody around except a few RVs and other vans."

"Good. Good. The girls?"

"Outside at the picnic table. I bought them some crayons and coloring books at the last stop. Anything to keep them occupied."

He nodded. It hurt to nod. It hurt to be awake. "Are they… are you okay?"

She rubbed her hands together. "I won't lie. I'm getting some aches and pains. A headache. Melody's not feeling so good, either. I was thinking, you know, maybe there's a clinic somewhere? Get ourselves tested?"

"Aw, shit. I never meant for this. I never wanted you guys to get sick. Go take care of yourselves. Forget about me."

"Enough of that. We already said."

"There's got to be something. Go to an ER. Get some of the good stuff."

Abeline shook her head. "There's no cure. Nothing helps. The hospitals are filling up. Old people are dying like flies."

"How old?"

"Real nice. You're a real charmer."

"What?"

"You calling me old?"

"I never did." He had run out of voice, run out of breath. "God, I'm tired."

"I don't know what else to do."

He opened his eyes again, shifted his body, trying to find some angle that would give him a little peace. "Got something to write with?"

"Do I? A pen?"

"You said the girls. Crayons. Paper. Get some."

She left for a few minutes. Slow Bear thought about dying. The problem with thinking about dying is that there is absolutely no way to imagine what not existing feels like. You always imagine your spirit floating around, watching yourself die, watching your loved ones bawl, watching your own funeral.

It ain't that, though. It's lights out. Like when you don't realize you fell asleep and jerk yourself awake? Without the jerking yourself awake part.

Abeline was back with the paper and Sunset Orange. Slow Bear sat still and tried to write on his knees without poking through the paper. It was a phone number. A name. *Oren.* He handed the paper to Abeline.

"What's this?"

"If I die, no, no, listen. If I don't make it, call him. Call him and tell him what happened to me. Tell him to help out with the girls."

"You're going to be fine. This is ridiculous."

"Just do it. If I die, get the fuck out of here. Go back home. Call Oren. Help these girls. Forget about me."

"Is that 'Oren'? Looks like 'Oral'. Wasn't that some sex-crazed preacher? Oral Roberts? Is this a one or a seven? Is that a three or an eight?"

He'd had about as much as he could of thinking straight and talking.

"Micah? You've got to have a good attitude if you want to get through this. Mind over matter. Pray or chant or whatever you want."

"Sure. Dear Sky King, heal my chakras. Blessed Father Eagle, grant me your strength." He started laughing.

"Shit's sake, boy. You'd better get better so you can fuck me again. How about that? Does that help?"

"A little."

"You know you liked it."

Couldn't help but grin. "Help me out of the van, how about it? I need you to get rid of this thing, get us a car from a newspaper. Something no one's looking for."

"I can't leave you here alone."

"Yeah you can and you will, and if I'm not here when you get back," he thumped the paper with his knuckle. "Call Oren."

Abeline helped him out of the van. It was a typical campground spot. Clear spot for a tent. Picnic table. Fire ring with a grate over it. Cut off from the other campsites nearby. She helped him to the table after she told the girls to get away, put their masks on. The forest floor hurt his soles, sharp sticks and pointy rocks. Hey, he was barefoot. Hey, Abeline was barefoot, too. He looked over at the girls – also barefoot.

"What happened to shoes?"

"Left them at the hotel. Couldn't find any at the truck stop."

"My feet hurt."

"Mine, too. There's nothing special about you on that."

Sat him down. He noticed the girls had left their coloring books and crayons. Looked like Pia was a real "inside the lines" type, trying to get the colors right. Melody just really liked green. It was all over the fucking place – picture of a Little Pony, the next page with a different pony, scrawled off the page and across the picnic table.

"Thanks, babe."

"Don't babe me."

"Get us some hotdogs, too. The girls have got to eat."

Abeline huffed and headed off. "Come on, girls. We're going to town."

Pia asked, "Are we leaving him to die?"

"I hope not. But if we are, I don't think it's his first time."

Slow Bear would've cackled at that if he didn't need that breath so bad for breathing.

CHAPTER 18

Abeline returned four hours later in a beat-to-fuck Chevy Cobalt with a loose belt.

Slow Bear had fallen off his bench and curled up on the forest floor, covered with dirt, ants and last year's dead leaves emerging from melting snow. Shivering with flushed cheeks. His wheezing was worse than the loose belt.

"Oh for the love of… Micah? Still with us Micah?"

"Yep."

"What are you doing down there?"

"Sitting up was hard."

She knelt beside him, helped him up and wiped crud and ants off him as best she could. His sweatshirt had a big wet spot where Slow Bear had drooled on it. His dreams hadn't helped this time. Most of them were about needing to take a piss.

He noticed she'd picked up some flip flops along the way, and for the girls, too.

"They didn't have any big enough for you."

"Okay."

The girls hung way back. Melody asked, "Did he get sick on our colors?"

"I'm sure they're fine." She set a couple of plastic grocery bags on the table and started unpacking – half-gallon of orange juice, no pulp, a gallon of water, cough drops (the gross menthol kind), hot dog buns, wieners, a can of baked beans, some paper bowls and plates, plastic forks and spoons, more cough medicine, giant bottle of generic pain killer…

Each new thump on the table made Slow Bear grit his teeth. Fucking headache, squealing like feedback from Dimebag Darrell's guitar.

"Girls, go get some long sticks, some strong ones."

Abeline pulled out a giant box of matches and a little tin flask of lighter fluid like you fill Zippos with. "Firewood's in the trunk."

"How much did you pay for the car?"

"Got him down under two grand. I needed that money, Micah."

"What did you do with the van?"

"Left it on a curb like, six blocks away from where I bought this. Did you hear me? I can't keep spending all my money."

"I already told you, leave me be. Go on home. Call Oren and tell him I owe you expenses."

"I'm not leaving you like this. You need the hospital."

He waved it off, nearly toppled off the bench again. "Don't need shit. I don't want to hear those goddamn doctors and nurses while I'm dying. Don't want the last thing I hear to be some beeping shit. Then what are they going to do with me? Study me on the slab? Put me in front of a med school class, give me a cute nickname like 'Mister Corpsey,' and show the students…"

He was going to say *Show the students my nasty fucked-up lungs* but he starting coughing and forgot how to speak, forgot how to think, and everything behind his eyelids went blinding white. He felt himself falling, but planted a foot down and coughed and stumbled. Couldn't see a goddamned–

Fuck, he slammed into the front bumper of the Cobalt, his shins vibrating pain down to his toes. He fell back on to his ass. Finally had enough of a break in the cough to suck up sweet, sweet hot-fudge-thick air.

"Micah?"

He couldn't talk yet. Still sucking air. He could feel his heart beat in his face, in his eyes.

"*Micah!*"

He forced one eye open.

Parked beside the Cobalt now, a giant, gleaming white Infiniti SUV with deep-tinted windows. Three people got out.

Slow Bear forced his other eye open.

Two men. One woman. All of them looked like pro wrestlers. All of them wore sunglasses. Two of them wore black leather jackets, with the last man in a wool sweater that looked like it had been through the wrong wash cycle.

None of them wore masks.

Abeline shielded the girls. The woman with the thugs – pretty thug-sized herself – waved her arms wide, like a goalie. "Whoa, whoa, whoa, hold up, it's all fine."

The guy in the sweater, bald and round all over, pointed at Slow Bear. "You Micah?"

Slow Bear nodded. Sort of. Too busy trying to hold in the coughs.

Sweater guy scratched his chest. Turned to the other man. "This is the guy."

"Shit. I think he's dying. Looks like we won't need to fuck him up. He's already there."

"Can't we put him out of his misery, then? I mean, we got the girls."

The woman standing in front of Abeline talked in a thick Boston accent. "Take it easy, there, easy. Nothing to be scared of, girls. It's all good, I promise."

She was blonde, her hair high and tight. A very broad back and thighs so thick with muscle, Slow Bear expected her yoga pants to Hulk-split at any moment.

Abeline stood her ground. "Stay put, girls."

"Hey, we've got a pool where we're going. Heated, too. You girls want to swim in our pool?"

Sweater guy's partner – got to call him something, so how about Plain Ugly? Anyway, this one was what happened to popular high school football players who got stuck in their hometowns, married to the homecoming queen he knocked up, stuck in a job that was supposed to be temporary, a diet of nacho cheese and light beer, plus thirteen years and a goatee.

Slow Bear shook his head. That sure enough became quite a story, didn't it?

Plain Ugly shrugged and took a couple steps towards Slow Bear. "Brian, want to help me drag him over?"

"Looks like you could do that on your own."

"What if he pukes?"

A shout from Abeline: "*He's got Covid!*"

Brian squinted at her. "Got what?"

"Covid! The virus! We've all been exposed!"

Plain Ugly took a step back. "Jesus."

"Now wait a minute–"

"You sure, Brian?"

"It's a hoax. Just a flu. You had a flu shot, right? Nothing to worry about."

"What is it, a hoax or a flu?"

"I'm just saying it's not bad, unless you're ninety years old."

Plain Ugly put his hands on his hips. "This dude's not ninety."

"Well, I don't know. Pull your shirt up over your nose. I'm telling you, though, it's fake news."

"Yeah," the woman said. "Fake news!"

Plain Ugly pulled his shirt over his mouth and nose, but it didn't stay in place. He and Brian each took a side as Slow Bear pushed himself up. The coughs came hard and fast, jerking him around like a puppet on strings. The thugs backed off. Slow Bear stumbled and jerked, finally draping himself across the picnic table, writhing on top of the supplies Abeline had bought. Squashing the buns, the wieners, knocking the cans off, making a huge mess.

"Micah!"

Abeline's voice.

"Fuck this."

Plain Ugly.

"We've got to. It's our job, man."

The blonde woman.

"Kill me, please."

Slow Bear.

This time, both Brian and Plain Ugly pulled their shirts up, each took a side, and dragged Slow Bear away from the table to the rear of the Infiniti, opened the back and threw him inside like he was luggage. Slammed the door.

Muffled girl shouts: "Micah! Micah! Micah!" and "Leave us alone!" and "Get your hands off–"

A slap. A yelp from Abeline.

Slow Bear went rigid, wished he had the strength. Sank back to the floor.

"Get in the back seat! Try that again, I'll rip your hair out. Go on! Climb in!"

Door opened. The girls, wheezy, trying not to cry. Abeline whispering to them, "It's okay. It's okay, I promise."

"Did they hurt Micah?"

Abeline's face, her cheek bright red, peeked over the back seat. "You okay?"

What little air made it to Slow Bear's lungs burned like a motherfucker. He gave Abeline a thumbs up.

Wherever they were going next wasn't going to be good. Might not even survive.

Fine with Slow Bear. He'd far outlived his expiration date, felt like cheese moldering in the back of the fridge. But for the girls and

Abeline, this was some wretched shit.

Golf clap from his papaw. *You still didn't bring my rum.*

The two thugs didn't bother searching him. Only touched him as long as it took to throw him inside. If they'd patted him down, they would've found the flask of lighter fluid and fistful of matches he'd shoved down the front of his sweatpants.

Hurt like hell, those sticks poking all over his balls, but better than nothing at all. Oh yeah, he was going to burn him some bad guys. Burn them real good, too.

As soon as he got over this virus.

Cough.

CHAPTER 19

Wheels on asphalt, Slow Bear's pounding head and wheezing, the girls' whimpers and whispers, Abeline comforting them, the blonde butch bitch telling them, "*Shut up, will ya?*" and the driver, Brian, on the phone to the boss, telling him what had gone down at the campsite…

Too much to hope for a quiet ride.

He cleared his throat. "Abeline?"

Her head peeked over again.

"Where… where… are we… huh?"

Then Melody's fingers and hair and eyes rose beside Abeline's face. "It's boring here."

"*I said shut up already.*"

"She's a kid. Let her talk. What's she going to do?"

Brian's voice. "How about everybody shut up? Even you, Darcy."

The blonde woman huffed and puffed. "What did I do? I'm doing my job is what I'm doing."

"If the kids talk, big deal, right? Calm down. It's not that big a deal."

"You're going to undermine me now? In front of everyone? It's because I'm a woman."

"I hear you, girl," said Abeline.

"Shut up, I said!"

Slow Bear closed his eyes. Counted to five. No, wait, four. Or eight. Try again: One, two, six, nine, six?

He opened them again.

Melody's fingertips, eyes and nose. An adorable "Kilroy was here." He grinned at her.

"Micah, where is Salt Lick City?"

"Salt Lick?"

"It's Salt Lake, honey," Abeline said.

"Would you both shut up?"

"*Shut up, Darcy! For fuck's sake!*"

"*Hey! You just drive, that's all you got to do, Brian. Drive, and let me deal with the–"*

"Salt Lake?" Slow Bear had planned on getting there on his own terms. "Don't drink the water."

"Okay."

"*We're not going to the lake.*"

"Is the city on the lake?"

"*No, how can a city be on a lake? That's stupid, kid.*"

"*Don't call her stupid, Darcy. You'd say a house is on a lake, what you mean is on the shore!*"

"*I swear, Brian–*"

And so on.

Probably headed straight to whoever it was Hampton told him about. Called his boss "empty," Slow Bear thought, which was weird. Took him a while, but realized he meant "MT." Initials. Some guy's name.

In Salt Lake City? Conservative Mecca? Mormon Disneyland?

This day couldn't get any weirder.

Slow Bear reached up, patted Melody's fingertips, then booped her nose.

He felt swooning and sick when the SUV exited the interstate and began turning at corners, swerving around bends, bumping through stop-and-go city traffic. Then everything slowed down.

Abeline's face appeared above Slow Bear. "We're in a gated subdivision."

"Hey, why can't you shut up? What the fuck?"

"Would you shut your cunt mouth? It's not like he can do anything about it."

"*Hey! Enough, you two!*"

Then the SUV came to a halt, and Slow Bear rolled around like a bag of groceries.

Doors opened, doors closed. That woman Darcy ordered Abeline and the girls to shut up again, but the girls chittered away. "I don't see a lake. But you said there was a pool, right? Can we see the pool? Why are we on the curb when the driveway is empty? Why does this house have so many roofs? Is it a castle? It looks like a castle."

The back hatch opened, and the sunlight stung Slow Bear's eye for a quick sec before Darcy and Brian grabbed his legs, gave them a hard yank. Slow Bear flew up and out before dropping straight down, smacking his head against the road. *Ah, fuck*! Last thing he needed on top of Covid was a concussion.

"Sorry about that." Brian crouched, helped him up. "You really don't look so good."

The bump on Slow Bear's head throbbed along with his heart. "You think?"

Once upright, another wave of coughing overtook him. "Jesus shitting Christ! Get me inside already, will you? Before I kill myself."

Brian took Slow Bear's arm, helped him up the driveway. Yeah, sure enough this might've been a castle in olden times, but now it was another McMansion in a long row of them, too many peaks, a three-car garage, lawns so perfect you could golf on them. A sloping walkway surrounded by dainty shrubs and one fake (surely, right?) marble fountain – three-tiered – led to the massive front door, mostly glass. A quick peek over his shoulder. It was odd. A flat, typically green suburban neighborhood, sprinkler on the lawn, backed by desert mountains and sky. Like a glassed-in colony on Mars.

Darcy led the way, Abeline and the girls behind her, then Plain Ugly, then Brian, holding up Slow Bear's coughing, limping frame.

The foyer, for fuck's sake, was something out of a magazine, if there was a magazine called *Homes With No Taste.* Chock full of chairs and mass-produced art and fake flower arrangements that didn't mean anything, all there because someone probably told the owner it should be. And of course, a grand staircase leading to a mezzanine. The walls were white with a pinkish buzz to them.

They rushed through to the dining room, past a giant table centered under a glass chandelier that must've weighed a whole cow, and then to the kitchen.

"We're back," Brian called.

The others moved over to the breakfast nook, pushed Abeline and the girls onto the bench seats. There were cookies on a plate in the middle of the table.

A man standing at an island in the center of the kitchen looked up, chef's knife in hand. He had a nice head of dark hair, some gray streaks on the temples. A full mustache. He wore a pullover polo and cargo shorts, leather sandals. Must be MT.

"Oh, look, they're all dressed the same. That's cute. Tell the girls they can have those cookies. You hear me, girls? It's Pia and Melody, right? Those cookies are all for you. Eat up."

Brian helped Slow Bear to the island so he could lean against it, then let go.

"And this is him?"

Brian nodded. "Micah Cross."

The man was cutting a chicken into parts. On cutting boards and in bowls around him were chopped carrots and onions and garlic, a lot of garlic, wood chips soaking. Tins of spices. A box of Kosher salt.

"Nice to meet you, Micah. Hope you don't mind, I've got chicken on me. I'm throwing all this on the grill later." He waved his knife around. "Anyway, I'm Miles Torn, and I'll be your Bond villain this evening."

Slow Bear coughed. Made sure it was a hard one, across all the food on the island. "What was that last thing?"

Torn's smile dropped, surveyed the damage. He looked up at Brian. "Is he sick?"

"He's got Covid!" Once again, Abeline's voice. Slow Bear couldn't help but grin in spite of the spit on his lips.

Torn pointed his knife towards her. It was like his magic wand. "Not so, ma'am. No, that's not what it is. Now, if it's the flu, or some sort of infection from all the abuse he's been taking, I can see that. But Covid isn't a real thing. I promise. Not at all. Right, everyone?"

The thugs agreed but looked nervous about it. There were a couple of new thugs in the kitchen with them – both white, both men, both smirking when the boss said Covid was bullshit. Both were in khakis and navy pullover sweaters, white Oxford collars rising from their V-necks. Slow Bear got a Sunday school usher vibe off them.

Slow Bear said, "Is that right?" Then coughed again. Harder.

"You know what they say, though. Fire cleanses. Stroke up a blazing fire in the grill, and *viola,* good as new. How many people do you know get sick from birthday cake? Just saying."

"You don't want the girls infected, though. Don't want to damage the merchandise."

The man *tut-tut-tutted.* "Show a little respect. They have names, and personalities, and will use everything they go through in life as a learning experience. Nobody *owns* them. Our client is renting their time, that's all. He'll feed them, clothe them, give them a place to sleep at night. Better than what you've been doing for them the last couple of days."

Torn went back to working on the chicken. He'd already sliced off one leg. Slow Bear thought, *I feel you, bird.*

"Bullshit."

"Please, step back." He got Brian's attention. "Can you wipe up the dirt he tracked in? Did you take his shoes?"

"He didn't have any."

Torn crinkled his nose. "That's gross."

"I'm gross? But you ship kids across the country for sex? This is some downright evil shit."

"No, not at all. It's business. I can think of a lot worse."

Made Slow Bear's stomach flip-flop, this smug bastard. "I can't."

"That's because you're not that smart. You're like, what, a bear. Yes, like a bear. You hunt, you kill, you eat. Doesn't matter what. Morality is straightforward to you. Anything that gets in the way of you hunting, killing, and eating is bad. Everything else doesn't matter. But humans are not bears. Humans are designed by God to do a lot more than just hunt, kill, and eat. Humans grow food when there isn't any. They *raise* animals, create a circle of life, rather than killing until everything is gone."

"Tell that to the bison."

"We *enjoy* our food. We maximize pleasure in it. We aren't mindless about it."

None of this was helping make whatever point he was trying to make. Slow Bear, distracted, checked out the new guards, wondered if they were good at their jobs or just fat, fascist eye candy. "That's one heavy load of horseshit you're hauling, man."

"See, sex is a spectrum. It's so much… richer, so much more complicated than you can understand. For a bear like you, it's about urge alone. You can't explain it. You just do it. Sometimes, you don't even put any thought into it. Like, with Miss Abeline here." He gestured the knife in her direction. She bit into a cookie. "A little old for you, not a good breeding stock, but your primal urge got the better of you to help satisfy a bodily function. Now you feel protective of her. All animal instincts, indeed. But imagine a more complex mind, and all of the different expressions of human sexuality. The Greeks and Romans–"

"Oh for fuck's sake, already!" Slow Bear coughed again. A grand cough. A sputum-spewing hack of mammoth proportions. He leaned closer to the food, too, coating as much as he could with spit and slime loaded to the gills with Covid.

Torn flipped the knife tip up to Slow Bear's chin and sliced. Slow Bear felt nothing at first, but then there was a sting. Fingers to his face. He pulled them away and saw blood, watched it drip to the floor and splat on his toes. He shook his head and wiped his hand on his sweatpants. "Cute."

Torn threw the knife onto the island. Disgusted. Hands on his hips. "My, I'll tell you what. If nothing else, you've got an asspocket full of gumption, yes indeed. I've been looking forward to this barbecue all day. I had a whole speech planned comparing you to each piece of chicken as I placed it on the grill. But now, Lord bless."

"What happened to 'fire cleanses all'?"

"Too late. Even I can't unsee this."

"Is he here, MT?" A voice booming on from the dining room. "Is he?"

A couple seconds later, a familiar face walked in. Not exactly "familiar" familiar. Giant bandage in the middle of the black guy's face, seeping red, with surgical tape wrapped around his head. Hampton took a look at Slow Bear and slowed his roll. "Aw, man, motherfucker looks like he's about to die. Who took his shoes?"

Torn crossed his arms. "He thinks he's got the virus."

"Does he?"

"No such thing."

"I told you already, that stuff is real. Why don't you get that?"

"This isn't the time or the place."

"I don't know how he went from Daredevil to *this* in two days unless it was Covid. He was stone cold. Took out everyone except me. Shot my nose off, man."

Slow Bear snorted. "Fuck you, I did not. That was your own guy."

"Really?" Torn raised his eyebrows. "Peter?"

"Yeah, but it was all this dude's fault."

"Well, he killed Gerardo, too. What am I going to tell their mother?"

"For reals?"

"*And* Lawrence *and* Spinner *and...*"

Slow Bear swooned again. Felt his forehead. Burning up. He hadn't caught the names of all the people he'd killed at the chicken joint or the motel. He thought of the woman with no face, still breathing. Shivers. He remembered now, though. "Petey." Thought of him as "Euro Trash."

Torn went on, "I liked Imelda. I was thinking of asking her out. She could've been wife number three."

Was Imelda the Greek or the other one? Slow Bear didn't care. "I'm going to be sick."

"Hampton? You want him, he's yours."

"I don't know, man. It's kind of pathetic, wanting to beat up on a sick guy."

Plain Ugly: "That's what I said."

"Then don't beat him. One shot, get rid of him. We're already a day late on the delivery. The guy's going to hold back late fees if we don't get a move on." He waved his hand over the contaminated feast on the island. "And we need something new to eat. Maybe ribs? We don't have time to cook now."

"Sure thing."

"Alright." He snapped his fingers at one of the guards. "You want to put in the order and pick it up? Get the whole spread."

Brian raised his hand. Like a schoolboy, seriously. Raised his hand. "What about the woman?"

Abeline.

Torn glanced towards the breakfast nook. "I don't know… I mean, *obviously* she's going to have to… you choose, okay? Take some initiative."

Slow Bear watched Abeline shrink in her seat and grip Melody a little closer. Too bad he was suffering, not thinking straight. Too many competing thoughts. Too much effort breathing. Too much, just too much, fuck, too fucking much.

Brian placed his hand on Slow Bear's back. "Come on."

Abeline's voice behind him. "Micah! Please, stay with me! Micah! Don't leave us!"

He turned to them. The woman thug, Darcy, held back Abeline. She kicked and scratched trying to get away, but Darcy ended up wrapping her arms around Abeline and carrying her out the door back through the dining room.

"Let go of me, you whore! You hear? I want to be with the girls! Get off me!"

No one said a word as her voice faded. Then Plain Ugly knelt beside the girls. "How about some TV, okay?"

Pia nodded towards Slow Bear. "We want to stay with Micah."

Plain Ugly almost looked sad. Made him twice as ugly. "Micah's not feeling so good. We're going to help him feel better. You guys, you like Nickelodeon? Or Disney Plus?"

The girls looked glum, Pia still studying Slow Bear for a clue. He let out a couple of coughs and nodded. "It's okay."

They climbed down from the breakfast nook and followed Plain Ugly's lead, corralling them out of the kitchen, hopefully to sit on a couch in front of a TV, left blissfully alone to watch cartoons or Baby

Yoda or whatever kids watched. Hands off. Slow Bear imagined smashing Plain Ugly's hands right then as he caressed Pia's shoulder on the way out. She shrugged it off. Good girl.

When they were gone, Slow Bear felt a crater in his chest, the feeling of falling through unlike anything he'd felt before. A free fall. An empty pain in the center of his wretched body, making him grit his teeth and groan, double over.

Brian said, "Come on, man," and carefully steered him towards the other kitchen door, leading to the back of the house. Hampton followed, slapped Slow Bear upside the head. "Payback's a bitch, motherfucker."

"Dude, I let you *live.*"

Another slap. "Aw, man, fuck that. If you hadn't gotten involved–"

"Does it hurt?"

Hampton's fingers reached for his bandage. Flinched. "They got me pumped full of some painkillers right now, but I can still feel it."

"Why the hell are you even here? Go back to the hospital."

Another slap upside the head. "Asshole, that's where all the sick people are."

"What about me? My germs are fucking your healthy cells right now."

An even harder slap. Slow Bear shouted out. Brian pushed Hampton back.

Hampton leaned in close. "I didn't think about that."

Torn busied himself throwing out his veggies and meat, mumbling the whole time – "Can't have a nice meal, can't have nice things, well, Jesus, what's the point?" – while his guard on the phone asked for ribs, brisket, coleslaw, baked beans and cornbread. And chicken. Plenty of chicken.

CHAPTER 20

The bedroom. Blackout drapes over the windows. Walls covered with eggshell cartons. Thick beige carpet. A single bed with a metal frame and plastic-covered mattress like at summer camp. A closet door. Slow Bear didn't want to imagine what was behind it.

The bed looked nice, though. Slow Bear was exhausted. He dropped to the mattress as soon as Brian let go. Started to curl into a ball, but Brian took his wrist and wrapped a leather restraint around it. Thick, black leather. Giant buckle. Perfect for BDSM.

Slow Bear sat up. "Let me be, man."

"Lay back. Ankles next."

He looked at the foot of the bed. Two more restraints hung from the frame.

"Look at me. Do I look like a flight risk? Do I look like… goddamn, I'm tired."

"I'm sorry, man." Brian, such a nice thug.

Behind Slow Bear, Hampton opened the closet door and clattered inside. "Don't apologize to that dude. He's fucking crazy."

"Maybe, but I can't help it. First I've seen of this virus up close."

"You believe it, then?"

"I don't know. MT says it's bullshit, but I mean, maybe it's something. How are we supposed to know? Those news people, they make it sound worse than it is. They do that to everything. Hurricanes, immigration, definitely Trump."

"Dude, I don't want to fuck with no diseases. Diabetes runs in my family. I don't want to risk it." Hampton closed the closet door and walked around the bed. He carried a toolbox, set it on the ground.

"But you're not wearing a mask."

"Those things don't work. The virus goes right through. You need a serious mask, one with a filter, but only doctors get those. In fact, I heard it on YouTube that wearing a regular mask raises your risks. You breathe in infected air, and it keeps collecting in the mask, giving you a bigger dose of virus."

Brian said, "Oh man."

"I know."

"Then why would the doctors say–"

"They can't admit they don't know what they're doing. They say what makes us feel better. But it's safer to not wear a mask, breath through your mouth more than your nose," said Hampton.

Slow Bear said, "Easy for you to say."

Hampton lifted his sneaker, kicked Slow Bear square on the knee. The pain was jackhammer bad. Slow Bear writhed and fell off the bed, started coughing again, twisting with his arm buckled to the bedpost. No way to steer himself.

He got his bearings back, spit on the ground. "Jesus, man, it was a joke. It was right there. I couldn't help it."

"Keep it to yourself, Raggedy Man." Hampton pointed to the toolbox. "Won't be funny when I go to work on you with my tools. So save your breath."

Brian looked skeptical. "Lay back and let me buckle your ankles, okay? Don't make us get rough."

"What if I start coughing bad? I'll choke on my own spit. I need some space."

Hampton tossed his head back. "Fuck this shit, man. We're not supposed to be nice to him."

"You want to fuck him up later or let him die on his own?"

"As long as he suffers."

"MT said we need some more information before we can kill him."

Slow Bear struggled off the floor, kicked himself upright before settling back onto the mattress. "Information? Me? I've got nothing to say."

"We'll see about that."

"I'm serious, though. What does he want to know? I'm an empty pot, y'all. The dregs in your can of beer."

"Shut up."

Brian's cell phone buzzed. He answered, mumbled, then hung up. "MT says food's here."

"So bind him up."

"How about, like, just one ankle?"

"Whatever. I'm hungry already." A glance at Slow Bear. "Those girls are invited, too. We're going to treat them so sweet, then they'll hop right into the car for the rest of the trip, happy as clams."

Slow Bear looked away.

Brian stretched out Slow Bear's right leg and bound it with the restraint. Nice and tight. He was half-off the bed, his free leg planted to keep his body from swaying like an empty hammock.

"We'll be back. You play nice and think of something to say." Hampton stabbed his middle finger in the air, then laughed and left the room, followed by Brian, who shrugged.

So.

His leg muscles, on the verge of spasms.

His arm, stretched so tight it might pop out of the socket.

A tool box full of torture devices.

A flask of lighter fluid and some matches digging holes in his crotch.

Slow Bear thought, *I've seen worse.*

CHAPTER 21

First – could he slip his wrist through the restraint? A few minutes of that was enough to answer *Fuck no.* These restraints were designed for comfort. Leather on the outside, but faux-fur lined the inside. Tight enough, but not cutting into the skin. Slow Bear imagined the sexual side of it, *wanting* to be tied up. What went on in a person's mind that made them okay with giving up control? Not Slow Bear. Trust issues up the wahoo.

If Slow Bear had a choice, his safeword would be, "Orange Juice."

That left him with his other foot, useless to help with the lighter fluid and matches.

But the toolbox.

Closed one eye, held his tongue right.

"Yeah, I can do that."

First attempt. He kicked out his leg but came short of the toolbox, planted it badly, bent his knee inward, the one Hampton had already smashed with his sneaker. That ratcheted up the pain. Slow Bear bit his lip until it bled to keep from crying out. He swallowed his blood the wrong way and started coughing again.

White flashes. Lost his mind. Stark raving.

The fever, that shit was *fierce.*

It felt like forever before he caught his breath, got enough strength to give it another go. He kicked out again, landed the front of his foot on the box and held on. He needed to hook it over the side and drag that thing over, but that was several inches out of reach. His skin slipped, squeaking as it stuttered off the top of the box.

Goddamnit!

How long did it take to eat a plate of barbecue, anyway?

The toolbox handle. Okay. If he could somehow get his toes under and lift it…

He was stretched as far as he could. Used his big toe.

Got it!

It fell.

Got it!

It fell.

Got it this time. Absolutely.

It fell.

Shit shit shit shit shit.

Try slowly. Lift just so. Try to shove his other toes in, and…

Got it!

Slow Bear flexed his toes up as far as he could and tried pulling the toolbox towards him.

Fuck. In'. Heavy.

His toes cramped, then slipped, then the handle fell.

"*Fuck!*"

Hanging there like a slaughtered pig.

Not true. Slaughtered pigs got more respect.

He held his breath, what little there was of it. Maybe that would do it. A light puff at a low candle. Hold it. Feel the darkness coming on. Feel the pressure. But he couldn't do it. He knew that. Worst you could do holding your breath was pass out, only for the simple part of the brain to take over with a sort of *The fuck is wrong with you*? Then it makes you keep breathing.

Keep living.

There you go. That's the meaning of life. Keep going. For no reason, no rhyme, no prize. Just keep going. Might as well be a fucking, what, like, a fucking *virus*. Ha ha. I know, funny shit right there. A little virus is all, "Keep going, man. Make more of us, and keep going. Then make some more and still keep going."

It doesn't stop for cigarette breaks.

It never takes a mental health day.

It doesn't even take a staycation.

Live and make more viruses.

Slow Bear got the living part. Had never bothered with the "make more" part. Lots of little Slow Bears running around, *play with us, play with us!* Then *feed us! Clothe us! Give us a place to live! Protect us!*

Another wracking cough.

He thought of babies. Helpless, hopeless babies.

He thought of Pia, a child with child. *Jesus.* And not in the religious way.

He thought of Melody, a tick in someone's ledger. He wondered how much the bastard in San Bernardino had paid for one that young.

How high would the prices go for kids younger than *that*?

And here he was feeling sorry for himself.

He kicked his foot out, lifted the handle, hooked it with his big toe, and focused every muscle, every thought, every breath on dragging that thing closer.

This time, it moved. Skittered across the carpet. Fell over on its side.

He pulled his foot from under it, scraping skin off the top of his toes. Kicked it upright. From there, it was a simple latch. Lifted up with his big toe. It didn't want to give. Took a shit-ton of pressure. Gritted teeth. Going to have to see a dentist one day, all the times he's gritted and ground them.

Pop.

The latch opened. Slow Bear's big toe dripped blood.

The rest would be easy, right?

He strained trying to see inside the toolbox. There was a tray on top, filled with a lot of sharp, poking things. Rusted things. Drill bits. Long thin knives. Screwdrivers.

He could work with a screwdriver. First, he had to knock the box over *again*, this time to spill out the tray.

Check.

Sharp poking things. Havoc on the sole of his foot. The blood was not helping him get a grip on any of the screwdrivers. Just got to squeeze one between his big toe and his–

This was fucking ridiculous.

Nobody would buy this. Some sort of Chinese acrobat contortions, but that takes years of training. Slow Bear was no way near limber enough, skilled enough, or healthy enough to pull this off.

But life keeps going. It defies expectations in order to do so.

It was a thick screwdriver, very long, very stained with god only knew what, rust orange spots. He lifted it with his foot, took a moment to breath, and watched it slip from his toes and clang off the bed rail and onto the floor. Out of sight, out of reach.

Desperate times, man. Desperate measures.

Slow Bear felt around on the floor. Something got him good and deep. He had to shake it free.

He found another screwdriver, picked it up by the handle. Smaller. Shorter. But he didn't drop it when he lifted it.

He couldn't cut the restraint around his other ankle. Couldn't gouge it with the screwdriver until it ripped apart.

Nope.

He had to thread the needle.

Leather strap, metal buckle. He slipped the screwdriver between the two and lifted. The effort made him want to throw up, but he swallowed the bile and kept on and on and on.

Until the strap began to move.

He kept pulling. Pulling. Pulling. Pulling.

The strap popped free of the buckle, but was still held in place on the other side by a metal rod.

He worked the screwdriver into the corner of the buckle. Carefully. Carefully. If he could make it stick, then drive the handle deeper with his foot…

But the screwdriver didn't hold. It fell away, clanged off the bedframe and out of sight, out of reach. Two for two.

This time he laughed.

Yes indeed.

This was some funny shit. Got this far only to fail *again.*

Fail *again.*

If Slow Bear was an expert at anything, it was failing. But he was bad at that, too.

Sure, that deserved a laugh.

It turned into a cough that made him feel muscles he didn't know he had.

Somewhere in that noise and pain, his papaw laughed.

Fuck you, kid. It was cute while it lasted.

"Fuck you, too, old man."

CHAPTER 22

"Alright."

Slow Bear rubbed his bloody foot across the plastic mattress, trying to wipe off the blood. He needed a good grip.

When he thought he'd gotten most of it clear from his toes, he reached up, gripped the loose leather strap between his strongest toes, and yanked it to the right as hard as he could. Hilarious. He pulled, slipped, pulled, slipped, pulled, slipped, pulled, slipped–

Cocksucker!

Slow Bear rubbed his foot against the mattress again, but this time scooted the elastic band around the end of his sweatpants up over his heel. Took a few tries. Then he pulled the rest of his foot inside.

This was the last play. None of the tools on the floor would do the job quickly enough. It was this or get tortured and killed, with no med school anatomy class waiting for him, either. No cute nickname. No final exams. Miles Torn in there would make sure every last part of Slow Bear disappeared into the Utah sand.

He covered his toes with the sweatpants, and went back to work on the buckle.

Would it work this time?

Pulled.

Slipped.

Of course it wouldn't. Haven't you been paying attention?

Pulled, slipped, pulled, slipped, pulllllllled, slipped. "Come on! Come on! *Cough* Fuck's sake!" Pulllllllllllllllled, slipped, pul-slipped, p-slipped, slipped, slipped, slipped–

Hold your tongue right and get it done!

Strained. Pulllllllllllllllllllllllllllllllllllled.

The rod released!

Then caught on the next hole.

That was all he needed. Pulled, slipped, pulled, slipped, pulled, slipped, pullllllled, the rod released again. Slow Bear toed it to the side quickly, slid the rest of the strap out and he was free.

His leg, anyway. Asleep on the bottom, cramped up top. He stretched it a couple times, but had to get to work fast. Took his teeth to the buckle around his wrist. Yes, much, much easier than the ankle. Much.

Got his hand free and it fell to his lap like spaghetti. Worried for a moment it wouldn't work at all. Shit. A one-armed man who couldn't use his arm was as useless as a no-armed man. He thought about wiggling his fingers. He pictured it. *Willed* his fingers to wiggle.

Three of them wiggled. Then all of them. Then the pins and needles hit like crazy, goddamnitall, and he shook his arm like it was covered in fireants, trying to force the blood back into place.

"Hey, Micah." He heard the voice a second before Brian rounded the door into the room. "Don't tell anyone, but I thought you would like–"

He stood in the doorway holding a big glass of iced tea. His eyes went nuts.

Slow Bear fell off the bed, face first on the ground. Lucky none of the sharp shit from the tool box stabbed him. No, wait, there it was. Like a dentist's hook or something, right into his chest.

He played dead.

Brian rushed for the bed and set down the glass of tea carefully. "Oh no, oh no, oh no. What the fuck? How did you, *shit*, how did you get out of… *shit*?"

Slow Bear kept still.

The matches, too, in his pants. Felt as if a couple of those had done some damage.

"Jesus Christ." Brian knelt beside Slow Bear, rubbed his back. "This Covid is going to kill us all."

Slow Bear couldn't hold his breath anymore. He burst out hacking then hacking more and there was the flashing white behind his eyes and wheezing and losing his marbles – who was he? Why was he here? Why wouldn't he die already?

"Aw, god, help me, please, god."

"Come on, let's get you back in bed. I'll go tell Hampton to lay off."

Same trick Slow Bear played back at the campground. While he was hacking his ass off, his hand was rooting around beneath him, looking for something, anything, to weaponize.

Felt like a very long nail. The type thugs used to hammer your ball bag to a chair.

Slow Bear rolled towards Brian and slashed up with the nail. Missed by inches, but threw Brian off his game. He hopped back. Fucker didn't have a gun with him. Sloppy.

He searched the floor – hooks and scrapers and drill bits and nails and hammers and *oh fuck* a little fucking ax.

Brian grabbed the ax just as Slow Bear got to his knees.

Whoosh. "Hey, Hampton! *Hampton*!" *Whoosh.*

Too close.

Slow Bear leapt at Brian, tackled him, and clamped his hand over his mouth, the nail still in his palm. Brian bucked and kicked and waved the ax around. One good thrust, and the ax bit into Slow Bear's ass cheek.

"No, man, no. Enough of that."

Slow Bear forced Brian's face to the side with his forearm, took the nail in his teeth, pushed it into Brian's ear, then let go and pounded it deep with his forehead.

The ax dropped to the carpet. Brian's mouth made an "O" and unleashed a motherfucking wail like you didn't want to hear, but Slow Bear kept the fucker's face smushed to the side, muffling the noise.

That had to hurt.

Not enough to kill him, though, which was the only way this escape was going to work. Slow Bear wanted that ax. If he wanted it, he would have to let go of Brian's face and reach for it.

Fuck it.

He lunged for the ax.

Brian sat up, both hands scrabbling at the nail sticking out of his ear as he sucked in a deep breath, ready to roar.

Slow Bear fumbled the ax, but then got a good grip, swung back and planted it in Brian's throat. It was a weak hit, Slow Bear drained and wrung out, but he tried again and again, Brian trying to block him, getting his fingers mauled, Slow Bear swinging harder and faster and angrier until he cut the artery and Brian gushed all over the walls and carpet.

He fell over. Done.

Slow Bear thought, *Goddamn, I need a nap.*

But that wasn't going to happen anytime soon.

He caught his breath. Maybe all this violence was doing him good. Some cardio to help fight the virus. Adrenaline pumping up the immune system. Dopamine – *yes, dopamine* – taking the slightest bit of pain away. Enough for Slow Bear to think straight for a beat or two.

The ax in his hand. Sure, it was good for one guy, but a roomful?

He turned to the mess on the floor. None of this shit was going to cut it. Little pokers and prodders, shit to slip under fingernails or punch into eyeballs or fuck with a man's balls, but nothing to scare the almighty fuck out of a room full of shit-stained kiddie-traffickers.

Wait a sec.

Drill bits.

Why the fuck would there be drill bits if there wasn't–

Slow Bear crawled to the toolbox. Only some of the tools had fallen out. Under the top tray, nasty hammers, ice picks, and a compact cordless drill. He picked it up, gave it a whir. Battery was powered up.

Oh shit (oh shit oh shit). Oh shit (oh shit oh shit).

Very glad he found this before Hampton had a chance to use it on him.

Another look around, and he found a big drill bit. Huge fucking drill bit.

He stood. Noticed the iced tea had been knocked over. He was parched.

"Well, fuck."

One last look around before he left. No, wait, he almost forgot.

Slow Bear set the drill down, then reached into his pants and pulled out the lighter fluid and some of the matches. He took the top off the flask, walked around the room spreading the fluid around, especially on Brian's corpse. Then he flicked a match with his thumb – glad he learned that trick – and tossed it onto the carpet.

Whoosh.

Another match. Another part of the room.

Whoosh.

Another match. Brian's corpse.

Whoosh.

That was a good start.

He picked up the drill.

"Here I come."

CHAPTER 23

The hall was clear.

Slow Bear emptied the rest of the lighter fluid halfway down the hall and flicked another match.

Whoosh.

"Aw, yeah."

The smell of the lighter fluid made Slow Bear shiver. The room he'd left behind poured smoke. The overhead smoke detector was quiet. Slow Bear guessed the batteries were long dead. But how long until the smoke reached the others?

He eased a peek around the doorway into the kitchen. Nobody there, but the island had been cleared and replaced with takeout trays, still half-full of ribs and chicken, slaw and beans.

Slow Bear made his way across the floor, slipped a couple steps on his own bloody footprints, set down the drill, and picked up a chicken leg, took a bite.

Was it feed a fever, starve a cold? Or the opposite? Didn't matter. The chicken did wonders for him. He ate a serving spoonful of beans. Damned tangy. Before choking on it all, he hefted a gallon jug of sweet tea and took a big swig. Gulped it down. Good stuff.

He covered his mouth with his forearm and coughed, hoping it didn't carry into the dining room, where it sounded like everyone was having a grand ol' time. A glance back at the hallway. Smoke began to roll out into the kitchen, spread across the ceiling. He grinned. It was a Covid miracle.

Time to get back at it. He picked up the drill and headed towards the dining room. It sounded like Darcy and Torn were trying to get on the girls' good sides:

"We've got brownies for dessert. You like brownies?"

"I bet you girls will like California. Movie stars, beaches, lots of little dogs, I'm sure you'll both get your own dogs. Any kind you want."

"After we eat, you can watch *Frozen 2*. Have you seen it yet? Are you more of an Elsa or an Anna?"

"I like Olaf!" Melody's voice.

Slow Bear's heart shrunk three sizes too small.

Pia asked, "Is Micah okay? I want to see him."

"You don't want to catch his flu, do you? He'd tell you the same thing."

"I want to see him."

Some other chatter, Slow Bear didn't know who: "My dad makes ribs better than this, but these aren't bad," "Soon as you're done taking out the garbage today, Hampton, I want you back at that hospital. We're going to get your nose fixed right away, better than before," "*Let it go, let it go.*"

Pia again: "I'm not going to get sick. We want to see Micah, and we want to see Miss Abeline."

"Eat your food, okay? Trust me, okay?"

"Anybody else smell smoke?"

That was Slow Bear's cue.

He rounded the door. That long table, every seat filled, even the new thugs from the kitchen, enjoying themselves some good grub. Slow Bear stepped up behind the chair closest to him – Plain Ugly's gnawing on a rib – and shoved the drill into the base of his skull.

Slow Bear pulled the trigger.

"Holy fuck!" Hampton leapt from his seat, knocked over his chair. Torn, at the other end of the table, stared with his mouth wide open, meat falling out. The girls screamed.

Once the drill bit was in, Slow Bear pushed harder, slammed Plain Ugly's head against the table. His arms and legs trembled.

Darcy and the other thugs went for their guns.

Slow Bear pulled Plain Ugly upright, kept pulling. His chair fell back and Slow Bear dropped to the floor beside it as the bullets cracked over his head. He yanked the drill from Plain Ugly's head after a few tough pulls, then crawled under the table, quickly, to where Torn sat frozen. As he started to push away from the table, Slow Bear drilled into his left kneecap.

A wincing scream from above.

Bullets aimed lower, kicking up splinters of hardwood floor around Slow Bear.

"*Stop! You'll hit me! You'll hit–*"

Too late. Torn's thigh exploded. Slow Bear braced his feet against the bottom of the chair and kicked back, still holding the drill. The bit tore free of Torn's knee. Slow Bear rolled out from under the table, slammed into Darcy's shins. She looked down, surprised. Swung her gun low just as Slow Bear raised the drill. Whirred it. Hoped it would distract her.

She shot him in the stomach.

Fuck you, Christ! That hurt!

He tangled his legs in hers and knocked her down. She dropped the gun. Reached for it. Slow Bear planted the drill bit through the center of her hand, into the floorboard. Then he let go of the drill, pushed himself and grabbed her gun.

Wheezing. Gut on fire. He yelled at the girls, "Get down here! Now!"

Pia and Melody slid from their seats, crouched under the table.

The leftover thugs were still shooting, getting closer. One of them got Darcy in the chest as she tried to stand. It was enough. She fell across Slow Bear, now on his back holding the gun over his head. Everything topsy-turvy. He aimed for the legs he thought were the thugs' and free fired until his mag was empty. *Click.*

His lungs were squeezed shut. He closed his eyes and tried to take in a deep breath. Deep was a pipe dream. Instead, he got himself a kiddie-pool breath. In out in out in out. He needed to check his GSW, but didn't dare drop the gun yet, even though it was empty.

Quick look around. One of the leftover thugs was on the ground. Good. The other had rounded the table, now standing over Slow Bear, pistol at the ready.

Slow Bear's pistol clattered to the ground. Too heavy. He started coughing again. *No! No! No!* The bullet in his gut made it a hundred times worse.

Flashing white.

Flashing white.

Flashing white.

Then, a shrill alarm sounded from the kitchen. Smoke detector, *finally.*

The thug shifted his eyes up, seeing the smoke for the first time.

Then there was the whir of the drill. The thug threw his head back, moaned at the ceiling, then dropped to his knees. Slow Bear turned his head. Pia, drill in hand, was destroying the thug's crotch. The drill bit hopped and jittered as she tried to get it to stick deeper. Melody clamped her hands over her ears and screamed almost as loud at the alarm.

Slow Bear grabbed the thug's wrist, tried to keep the gun pointed anywhere but at him or the girls. The thug fought. Slow Bear could only hold on a few seconds, but it was enough for Pia to climb out from under the table and drill into the middle of the thug's spinal cord. He twisted left and right, trying to shake her off, reaching behind his back, firing a shot that missed Pia by inches. She shrieked but kept her finger on the trigger, kept on drilling.

Slow Bear took a swipe at the thug, slapped him across the face. Too weak to keep it up. Lucky that the thug went slack, his gun arm falling across Slow Bear's body. Then the rest of him.

Pia let go of the drill. Melody stopped screaming. The smoke detector in the kitchen stopped – probably burned up – but the one in the dining room picked up where it left off.

Slow Bear thought this was it. Gutshot, dying of Covid, about to burn up in a Mormon McMansion.

"Pia, listen, Pia, listen to me. Where's Abeline?"

"They took her to the basement."

"Think you can go find her?"

"I'm scared, Micah. Please get up and go with us."

"I… I need a few minutes. I promise, just a few minutes. Go see if you can find her. Is there anyone else in the house?"

"I don't know."

"Shit. No, wait, it's okay. Go see if you can find her. I'll watch Melody."

"Micah–"

"You've got this. Take the drill with you. It'll be okay. Hurry."

She leapt to her feet and ran off. Melody sat beneath the table, shaking. Slow Bear motioned her over. "It's… alright. Come here. It's going to be fine."

"Yeah, little girl. It's going to be just perfect."

Hampton's voice.

Slow Bear looked toward his feet, the kitchen door. So much black smoke now. Hampton stood several feet away, goddamned AR-15 in his hand.

Jesus, America, all these guns.

Good thing Slow Bear took one from the thug, but now his hand was tucked under his ass and he didn't have the strength to lift it.

Hampton was breathing hard. "Aw, man, how do you do that with only one arm?"

Melody scooted over to Slow Bear's side.

"Little girl, come over here with me, and we'll go get your friends. Micah is a bad man. He wants to do bad things to you. You and me both. But I can take you out of this, take you somewhere safe." He took a step closer, took one hand off his gun, beckoned her. "Take my hand. Come away from him."

The girl tightened her lips and furrowed her brow. She leaned over Slow Bear, putting herself right in the path of the bullet, keeping her eyes on Hampton. "No."

"You need to move, girl."

Slow Bear pulled in enough breath to say, "Melody, please. Get out of the way. Go on. Go find Pia and Abeline."

"No, Micah. He won't shoot me. You know he won't."

"Please, get out of here."

"Come here, little girl. I promise. I double-promise. I'm going to take you someplace safe. Micah is a bad man, a real bad man."

Slow Bear thought, *How do you live with yourself?* Fucker drives kids around, delivers them to pedos, and still has a health plan? Shit.

"No! You leave Micah alone! He's a good guy!"

Hampton took a step closer, hand still reaching for Melody. "He's not. I swear. Let me help you. We'll go find, uh, Pia, and uh, your other friend. I promise everything's going to be okay."

Melody didn't move. "Get away from us!"

He was really close now, at Slow Bear's feet, leaning over, gun barrel looking more and more like surefire death while Hampton's other hand grasped for Melody's arm. He got a grip. She screamed, "*No, I said, no, I said no!*" Pulled back. But he had her, started to wrench her away from Slow Bear.

Slow Bear grunted, pulled his hand free, flopped his arm up, barely able to support the weight of the gun.

"Oh shit!"

Hampton hopped back.

Slow Bear fired a shot before his arm fell to his crotch.

The bullet struck Hampton somewhere, hard to tell where. Like he absorbed it.

He fell on his ass, legs splayed, but still fired back. The bullet sliced between Slow Bear and Melody – a little too close to the girl. She scrabbled across Slow Bear and grabbed his gun hand, covered his trigger finger with a few of her fingers, and squeezed.

Wasn't pretty. Wasn't straight.

Melody squeezed again and again. Two more wayward shots.

Hampton held his forearms over his face like a boxer on defense. "Hold up, wait, hold up!"

Slow Bear steadied the gun. Angled it up a bit.

Melody squeezed again.

Hampton sagged, fell onto his back.

Slow Bear lifted his head, teeth chattering, waiting for Hampton to rise again and end it all for them.

But he didn't.

"Did I kill him, Micah?"

Shit, she didn't need that on her mind. "It was all me, kid. You gave me a little help is all. It's okay. He was a bad, bad man."

"I know."

Thick black smoke. Flames whooshing in the kitchen. Melody started to cough.

"Micah, I'm sleepy."

"Me too."

Helluva way to die. He could only imagine what the Devil in Hell had planned for him, letting this precious girl die alongside him.

"Micah?"

He looked up.

Pia.

"Get up. We need you."

CHAPTER 24

Melody and Pia helped Slow Bear sit up. They kept pulling and prodding, begging him to stand. The bullet in his gut begged him to stay the fuck down.

So easy for kids. Resilient little cusses.

Pia rattled on the whole time: "I found Miss Abeline downstairs, but the door is locked and she can't come to the door because she's tied up and we need to go help her, come on Micah, come on, please, please, hurry."

Felt like they were pulling his arm out of socket.

He shook them off. "Give me a second."

"We don't *have* a second! Hurry! Look, there's a fire!"

"I know! I set the fire." A deep breath. Fucking hell. "Okay, here we go. One, two–"

Slow heaved himself off the ground, wobbled, and a flash of pain lit up his nerves like lightning. He ended up on one knee.

"Four, five–"

That time he made it all the way. Lightheaded. Felt like gravity was gone.

"Lead the way."

Pia wrapped her arm around Melody's shoulders and helped her along as Slow Bear followed. Watching her take care of the younger girl gave him the strength to go on, even if he had to find the wall first for support. Slumped his bad shoulder against it so he could keep hold of the gun in the other. Like it mattered. Between him and the thug, fuck only knew how many bullets were left. At least one, for sure, since the slide hadn't racked back.

Pia looked back and shouted, "Hurry! Hurry up!"

"Wait a sec, give me a minute." He remembered they didn't have a way out of here. Fire department would be coming soon, and cops too. Even if they made it out of the house, the best they could do is wait around for the authorities, which would land Pia and Melody right back in the system. Fuck that noise. He made his way to Hampton, eyes still open, still moving around. Not dead yet.

"Don't make me shoot you again."

Hampton weakly grabbed for Slow Bear's hand as it checked the not-dead man's pockets until he found his key fob.

Hampton finally grabbed hold. "Aw, man, this blows."

"You don't have to tell me."

"Aw, man."

Slow Bear twisted his hand from Hampton's grasp, then turned and limped away.

The basement door. The girls waiting for him. More smoke here than he had expected, the fire spreading too fast. He thought he'd have them all out of the house by now, but then it went to shit.

Pia told Melody to head down the stairs. She lingered a moment until Slow Bear made the first step. "I can help. Hold on to me if you think you'll fall. We need to hurry."

Each step, a jackhammer, a micro-blackout. Felt like half a day to make it all the way down, but it couldn't have been more than a couple minutes. Pia there, guiding him. At the bottom, he looked around – a furnished mancave, with shag carpet and wood panels, a leather sectional, theater seating, a digital projector and screen, fancy red pool table, and a gun rack on the wall, some hunting rifles and a couple of shotguns. Useless to a one-armed man.

Pia pointed towards a wooden door. "She's over there. I think it's a bathroom."

Slow Bear walked over, pounded the pistol butt on the door. "Abeline? Hey, Abeline?"

Muffled: "Micah?"

"You okay in there?"

"No! No, I'm not! Of course I'm not!"

He shoved the pistol into his waistband. The weight dragged his sweatpants off past his butt. So he grabbed the piece, handed it to Pia. He tried the doorknob. Locked. It was cheap, and any other day he would've probably twisted it until it broke, easily. The door, too, probably easy enough to kick through on a good day. But now, might as well have been a bank vault.

"Can't unlock the door?"

"They tied me up. I can't do jackshit."

Slow Bear leaned against the door. Almost slipped into a nap. Felt like he was very near his last breath, to tell the truth.

"Give me that." Held out his hand to Pia. She gave him the pistol. "Hey, Abeline, are you in front of the door?"

"I'm on the ground, face first."

"Okay." Slow Bear stuck the gun barrel against the door, between the knob and jamb, angled it up. "This might hurt a bit."

The *pop* of it surprised him. Louder down here than in the dining room, where there had been several guns going off. The girls shrieked and covered their ears. Scared Slow Bear for a second – he thought maybe the bullet had ricocheted, but no. They were fine. He looked down at the gun, slide now racked back. It was done. He tossed it aside, pushed open the door.

Abeline was hogtied with zip ties, extra tight, cutting into her wrists and ankles, connected by another in the middle. It was a cramped space, hardly enough room for the toilet and sink, but they'd managed to contort her to fit. Her cheek crushed against the far wall.

Slow Bear dropped to his knees beside her.

"Micah, thank god." She craned over her shoulder. One eye was swollen shut, bruised dark all around. Her mouth, too, bloody and bruised. "Thank god. Wait, are you bleeding? Jesus, Micah."

He looked around the bathroom. He needed something sharp, and fast. On the sink? Nothing. In the cabinet beneath? Abeline was in the way. He couldn't open it.

"Micah, there's smoke out here!" It was Pia.

"Smoke? Jesus, what's happening? Tell me they didn't shoot you, please, Micah, tell me."

Slow Bear shook his head. "Can't tell you that. Pia, go get the gun again."

She did, brought it over. He held the top slide. "Push that right there, see? Push hard. Yeah, good. Push it again, hold it down, and pull the bottom of the… yeah, like that."

The gun slid apart. Slow Bear shook the barrel and spring out, ran the rail over the connecting zip tie. It wasn't working.

"Pia, come here."

He had her hold the rest of the frame under the zip tie, sawed the damned thing with the top slide. The plastic began to give way, and then it snapped. Abeline let out a moan as her legs dropped and her body straightened again. Pia and Slow Bear tried the same thing on her ankles and wrists – couldn't help but cut through her skin, but it worked, and Pia helped Abeline to her feet.

"Oh god, I'm so glad you're okay. Melody! Melody, come here, sweetie!"

The younger girl ran into the bathroom and slammed into Abeline's legs, nearly toppled her over, but held on tight. Slow Bear stood slumped against the doorjamb, head lolled back.

"My god, Micah, my god, my god."

He grinned at her. "No big deal."

"We've got to get you out of here."

"You guys go ahead. I've done about as much as I can do."

She rose on her tiptoes, still too short for face to face, and placed her palms on his cheeks. "It's time to leave."

He shook his head. "No, really, let me be. The girls… don't let the cops take them. You understand?"

"Snap out of it. Let's go."

"You still got that number I gave you?"

"What? Micah, please."

"That number, I wrote it down for you. Remember his name?"

"What, Oral? Was it Oral?"

A smile with teeth for once. "Oren. Remember Oren. Do you have the number?"

She checked her sweatpants pockets, found the paper, and showed him.

"Call him. I mean it. Call him as soon as you can. But get out of here."

More smoke flooded into the basement. Pia, at the foot of the stairs, covered her nose with her shirt collar. "I can't see the top anymore!"

Abeline threw her arm around Slow Bear's waist and forced him to walk. She pulled him towards the stairs. She had to pull her shirt up over her nose, too. "Pia, when you get up there, drop and crawl towards the front door. Make sure Melody is with you."

Pia helped Melody up the stairs in a scurry, while Abeline coaxed Slow Bear along. "Lift your foot. One step at a time. We've got this."

He grew heavier in her arms. "I can't. Go on. Listen, in my pocket." He slapped his hand on his opposite jeans pocket. "Keys. Take these keys."

"Come on. The first step is the hardest. I can't hold you up anymore. Don't give up on me."

"I'm not giving up. I finished the whole thing. This is it. Let me down."

"Fuck you, Micah! Fuck you for doing this to me. Go up these goddamned stairs with me, you piece of shit!"

"Set me down. I'm serious."

Abeline strained to keep him up, but her strength finally gave out, and Slow Bear fell, his back against the wall and his legs splayed on the stairs. He slapped his sweatpants again. Abeline ducked, the smoke now burning her eyes, making them run tears. She pulled out the key fob. Turned back to Slow Bear.

He looked beyond pain, blissed out. Stupid grin on his face.

"Go on, now."

She shook her head. "You're a real asshole, you know that?"

"You're welcome, bitch."

She leaned in, pecked him on the cheek, then climbed the stairs.

Halfway up, Abeline looked back, but through the smoke could only see the man's feet.

CHAPTER 25

Through the smoke, out the front door, onto the walkway.

Fire truck sirens, closer and closer.

The yard filled with neighbors, many recording with phones.

Of course they are.

Abeline gathered the girls under her arms, told them to walk fast, don't say a word to anyone. All three of them coughing.

Neighborly concern: "Are you alright?" "My god, what's going on in there?" "Do you work for him?" "Are you his wife? I didn't think he had a wife." "Just sit down. The ambulance is on the way."

Abeline told them "No, thank you, no," but they followed as she walked the girls down to the street, clicking the key again and again and again *click click click.*

They must've looked scary – Abeline beaten and bloody, the girls greasy with smoke and other people's blood.

A Suburban across the street on the curb a couple of houses down beeped when she hit the button. So there it was. Gangsters and their SUVs, right?

Neighborly concern turned to anger on a dime. It was a goddamned mob. "Where are you going? The police are coming. Come back! Hey, come back! Stop it. Hey, hey, lady, where the hell–"

Crowding in front of her, phones recording, blocking her path. Abeline grabbed a phone from some bitch's hand, flung it over her shoulder. Shoved another man out of her way.

"Record her! Get the license plate!"

Oh yes, they had to do their civic duty, snapping the Suburban's plate, looking smug as warm shit about it. They hoped it might go viral.

"Get back. All of you." Abeline opened the back door and helped the girls inside. Closed it. A woman Abeline's age, but wearing it a lot worse than she was, hovered over her shoulder, phone at arm's length. Abeline spun on her, grabbed her wrist and twisted hard.

"Hey, you're hurting me! Assault! Assault!"

Abeline twisted harder until the woman dropped to her paper thin-skinned knees.

That got the phone crowd really riled up.

Fuck it.

Abeline climbed in, cranked up, and pulled away.

She drove past two screaming firetrucks. How far behind were the cops?

It didn't matter. All she cared about was the road ahead. Tried hard to shake Slow Bear from her mind. Stupid man. Stupid, *stupid* man. Realized she was holding her breath. Very stupid man. Let it out slow. How long since she'd had a cigarette?

Goddamn it! What was she supposed to do now? How did she end up like this?

The girls clung to Abeline, bunched up between the two front seats, still shaking and coughing, staring out the windshield. A while later, they let go and fell asleep on the bench seat.

Hundreds of miles to drive. No cops in the rearview. No phone, no purse, no ID, no money. Once they made it home, if she *did* make it home, Jesus, the consequences.

Another glance behind. Melody's head in Pia's lap, both sound asleep.

The fuck was she going to do with these two girls? She'd already raised two adult children. She had grandchildren. Her mothering days had been over for a long time. She enjoyed her freedom. Barhopping, drinking, having some fun with men. Being a grandma every now and then was fine.

It didn't matter what Slow Bear had said. Slow Bear was dead. The girls would be much better off with professionals. You know, like, therapists and shit.

Anyway, not the right time to think about it. One day at a time. Fuck, one *hour* at a time. They were still far from home.

Truck stop in Colorado. After Midnight.

Abeline searched through the center console, the door side pockets, and the glove compartments, scrounging together enough change to buy a coffee, help keep her awake.

A pay phone mounted on the outside corner of the building caught her eye. Don't see those much anymore. She jiggled the change in her hand. Micah had been serious about calling his friend Oren. Was it worth it to call now, or get the coffee, get back on the road, and call when she got home?

She didn't want to take any chances.

The phone still worked. The handset was sticky. She plunked in her money and dialed.

Three rings.

A light and festive voice answered. "Yes, please?"

"Is this Oren?"

A long pause. "Why in the world would you call here looking for *Oren*? Who the hell is Oren?"

"So, this isn't Oren?" Abeline looked at the number again.

"Who is this?"

"Who are *you*?"

A sigh, "Listen, ma'am…"

"Micah Cross gave me this number."

"Who?"

"His name is Micah. That's what he told me, anyway."

"I'm sorry. I wish I could–"

"He was a one-armed Indian."

"Wait." The voice lost its fun edge. "That's Slow Bear. That's got to be Slow Bear."

"He said his name was Micah Cross."

"He says a lot of things. Last I saw him, he looked like death warmed over, except for his eyes. His eyes were clear. Is he with you? Can I talk to him?"

"Um… I think he's dead."

Abeline spilled everything that had happened. She needed to tell *somebody*. She kept her back to the sliding glass doors, but peeked over her shoulder to make sure the girls were still safe in the Suburban.

When she was done, Oren cleared his throat. "Dead."

She wiped the wet from her cheeks. "Mm hmm."

"I'm very goddamned sorry to hear that. I truly am."

"So what do I do? Please, tell me."

"I want you to go home. Do exactly what Slow Bear told you. Tell the police your car was stolen, your purse inside. Get a haircut, and a different color. And don't do anything else until you hear from me."

"When will that be?"

"Soon, trust me. Don't call this number again. It won't be in service. By-ee."

He hung up.

Abeline didn't feel any better. But at least the cold air and the conversation had made her more alert.

She climbed back into the Suburban, started driving, and stayed awake all night, all the way back to Nebraska.

The Escalade Micah had driven was no longer parked on her curb.

She pulled into the driveway, late morning. Only junk mail in the box. She'd only been gone for a few days but it felt like so many more. She took the girls inside and the three of them crashed on Abeline's bed, fully dressed, still dirty and bloody, for the next twelve hours.

Abeline called the police. She told them her car and purse, all her cards and ID, her cell phone, all stolen. She called Visa and Discover and Shell and Macy's, a few other companies she could remember, and canceled the cards. Canceled her cell phone service.

Started over.

Cleaned and fed the girls, still shell-shocked. She hoped a little more sleep and peace would bring them around soon.

Found some hair dye in the back of the bathroom cabinet. She'd gone brunette for a man once. He didn't stick around long, and she switched to red. This time was different. She twisted some strands, looked in the mirror. Maybe it was time to go grey. All she had to do was nothing, wait a year. Always thought it would make her look old.

Didn't matter. Time to accept it. Since the cops would be looking for a redhead, though, she needed a faster change. Brunette was fine for now. She also had Pia bunch it into a tail and cut it off at the nape of her neck. Not the best style, but enough until she could get an appointment with her stylist, after this Covid shit went away.

A FedEx man rang the doorbell, handed her a medium-sized box. After he drove away, Abeline sat at the dining room table and opened the box while the girls watched TV.

Birth certificates. Adoption papers. New names for the girls. Paperwork that showed step-by-step how they had come to be with Abeline. Medical records. School transcripts.

"Holy shit."

They looked legit. There was absolutely no way they could be, but there was no way to tell.

Also in the box: a credit card in her name. Title for the Suburban she'd stolen, plus new plates.

And: fifteen thousand in cash.

The last piece of paper, handwritten from Oren. A list of instructions – who to call, what to say, how to pass muster, in order to keep the girls.

If Abeline could do it all over again…

Okay, she still would've fucked him. That was a real good time.

But when he showed up again the next day? You better fucking believe she would've cursed him up one side and down the other. She would've beat Micah's chest until it was purple and black. She would've kicked him out and told him to forget she ever existed, and *take the girls with him*!

But one look at Pia and Melody on the floor in front of the TV watching *Bob's Burgers*, Melody thumping the older girl's ear every now and then, raising a "Quit it!" from Pia, made Abeline forget why she was so mad.

Sort of.

She followed Oren's list to the letter.

She told her own kids why she'd taken in two orphans without discussing it with them first. Oh god, that sucked. They were *pissed*, but they'd get over it. It wasn't like there was some sort of inheritance for them to worry about. All the money was on their dad's side.

She made an appointment for Pia with Planned Parenthood. Drove over to the big city, did what had to be done, and then grabbed some Chinese takeout on the way home. Neither of the girls had ever eaten Chinese food before. They loved it.

She could wait on enrolling them in school. The Covid quarantine put a hold on that.

As the weeks went by, well…

There were still nightmares. All three of them. But their bodies healed, the fear faded, and things got really boring really fast.

New names for the girls on the paperwork – Lisa and Katherine. They couldn't remember who was who. Neither could Abeline. The girls liked their own names, so that's what she called them, but told them to think of "Lisa" and "Katherine" as characters they had to play, like in a movie, but this time in real life. Pia had already learned a lot about lying, was getting too good at it, which worried Abeline to no end.

Pia especially hated Abeline acting like their mother. There were many arguments, raised voices, "*I hate you!*" Many apologies. Many tears.

One time, Abeline asked Pia – "Katherine," no, "Katie" –

pointblank, "Are you fine with this?"

The girl shrugged. "It's okay."

Good enough. What more could be said.

Then there was the virus. Abeline ended up sick after all. She got a pretty bad case, but swore not to go to the hospital, worried about what might happen to the girls. She held on, Pia taking care of her, and after two weeks began feeling better.

Pia and Melody? No symptoms at all.

About a month later, Abeline went out to the mailbox. The usual junk, the usual bills and credit card offers, some new cards finally arriving to replace the old ones, a letter from her daughter's lawyer boyfriend – cheating on her husband with him, a lot of nerve having him write her – threatening all sorts of bullshit trying to get Abeline to give up the girls. Yadda yadda.

And a postcard. Abeline didn't think people sent postcards anymore.

On the front, "Greetings from *San Bernardino*" in vintage letters, each one a new scene from the city, and also a train, some orange trees, and mountains.

She flipped it over. Splashed with something brown, dried out. Blood, a good guess. A partial fingerprint. Other than her address, there was only one line:

Wish you were here.

She closed her eyes and smiled.

"What an asshole."

THE END

Acknowledgements

In addition to all the literary "Jims" (Crumley, Burke, Ellroy, Harrison, and Thompson), I was also visited by the worn-down muse of Ted Lewis this time. Goddamn, what they could all do with a sentence.

Thanks to the support of Chris Black at Fahrenheit 13 and Chris McVeigh at Fahrenheit Press, and to all my Fahrenheit author friends brought closer together due to this disease that kept us apart. Cheers.

Thanks to Victor Gischler and Sean Doolittle for being there, for over twenty years now. Whatever craziness happens to me in this business, they're usually the first to know. Love you guys.

Apologies to Brian Koppin for using his name for Brian the thug and then killing the living shit out of him.

Everything I do, I do it for Brandy, Lorna, Herman, Myrtle, and Lucille.

Hi, Mom (Sandi), and Linda (Mother-in-law). Hugs and Kisses.

By the same author.

- *Slow Bear*
- *The Butcher's Prayer*
- *Trash Pandas*

About the author

Anthony Neil Smith is the author of numerous crime novels, short stories, and essays. He is an English Professor at Southwest Minnesota State University.

He likes British beer, Mexican food, and Italian crime flicks from the 70s. His newly adopted dog is named Edmund, and he is the devil.

You can find out more about his work on his website www.anthonyneilsmith.com.

More books from Fahrenheit Press

Know Me From Smoke by Matt Phillips

Stella Radney, longtime lounge singer, still has a bullet lodged in her hip from the night when a rain of gunfire killed her husband. That was twenty years ago and it's a surprise when the unsolved murder is reopened after the district attorney discovers new evidence.

Royal Atkins is a convicted killer who just got out of prison on a legal technicality. At first, he's thinking he'll play it straight. Doesn't take long before that plan turns to smoke—was it ever really an option?

When Stella and Royal meet one night, they're drawn to each other. But Royal has a secret. How long before Stella discovers that the man she's falling for isn't who he seems?

"A beautifully written, brutal & brilliant slice of hardboiled crime fiction. A Knockout."

Pure by Jo Perry

Caught in a pincer movement between the sudden death of Evelyn (her favourite aunt) and the Corona virus, Ascher Lieb finds herself unexpectedly locked down in her aunt's retirement community with only Evelyn's grief-stricken dog Freddie for company.

As the world tumbles down into a pandemic shaped rabbit-hole Ascher is wracked with guilt that her aunt was buried without the Jewish burial rights of purification. In order to atone for this dereliction of familial duty, Ascher – in her own words 'a profane, unobservant, atheist Jew, frequent liar and grieving loser' –volunteers to become the newest member of Valley Haverim Chevra Kadisha, a Jewish burial society on-call twenty-four-seven during lockdown and performing Mitzvot at no cost to the bereaved.

What follows is a journey through the insanity of lockdown in Los Angeles as Ascher attempts to bring peace to a troubled soul, and perhaps in the end redemption for herself.

'The mystery will get under your skin, for sure, but the humanity of this novel will resonate far beyond the page."

Turbulence by Paul Gadsby

Accidentally shooting a civilian during a bungled heist was bad enough, but when they upset the local criminal kingpin as a result of their ineptitude, newbie bank-robbers Birty & Cole figured the best thing to do was split town, and fast.

Smart plan - at least it was till everything went south, again.

An armed robbery is an unusual event which affects the lives of everyone touched by it and in this tour de force Paul Gadsby traces the lines of influence and connection that run through the lives of the people unwittingly caught up in Birty & Cole's heist.

The story is woven through the lives and perspectives of many characters - everyone from the bank staff and customers who witnessed the raid, to the journalists covering the case.

This remarkable novel from Brit-Noir legend Paul Gadsby ignores the usual crime fiction tropes of 'robbers on the run' and instead becomes a vivid study into cause & effect that will keep you gripped until the very last ripple fades away.

"Gadsby has really come into his own with this book - the writing & the storytelling are simply superb."